BANISHED

BATTALION BANISHED

DEFENDERS OF THE OVERWORLD

BOOK 2

Nancy Osa

Living to fight another day . . .

Sky Pony Press
New York

First Edition

This is a work of fiction. Names, characters, places, and incidents are from the author's imagination, and used fictitiously.

Sky Pony Press books may be purchased in bulk at special discounts for sales promotion, corporate gifts, fund-raising, or educational purposes. Special editions can also be created to specifications. For details, contact the Special Sales Department, Sky Pony Press, 307 West 36th Street, 11th Floor, New York, NY 10018 or info@skyhorsepublishing.com.

Sky Pony® is a registered trademark of Skyhorse Publishing, Inc.®, a Delaware corporation.

Minecraft® is a registered trademark of Notch Development AB. The Minecraft game is copyright © Mojang AB.

Visit our website at www.skyponypress.com.

10 9 8 7 6 5 4 3 2 1

Library of Congress Control Number: 2015941431

Cover illustration by Stephanie Hazel Evans
Cover design by Brian Peterson

Print ISBN: 978-1-63450-997-8
Ebook ISBN: 978-1-63450-999-2

Printed in Canada

Just for Ken

BATTALION BANISHED

CHAPTER 1

HOW STRANGE IT FELT TO HIKE ALONG IN THE open, Frida thought, where any griefer, sorcerer, or other hostile could attack at any moment. The longtime survivalist shook off her natural tendency to hide, yet remained on guard. She had to appear unworried and assume her new identity—a subordinate to Lady Craven and the criminals who were terrorizing the Overworld.

Somehow, human griefers had obtained the magic to withstand normal injury and to enchant dangerous mobs to do their bidding. Although Frida's commander, Captain Rob, had managed to slay the powerful Dr. Dirt, his next-in-line—Lady Craven—had absorbed Dirt's power and become even more fearsome. The sorcerer was continuing to systematically take over biome after biome by using her undead legions to threaten innocent citizens. *Not if I can help it*, Frida thought grimly.

She walked briskly toward the plains boundary, trying to act comfortable in the borrowed gray skin that masked her olive-green coloring and family tattoo. Her usual camouflage clothing had been replaced with a red and white jogging suit, and her dark hair was encircled by a terrycloth headband—*So not me*, she reflected with a slight grin. But the costume would help her infiltrate the griefers' hillside encampment and, hopefully, find a way to help her battalion overcome their evil zombie and skeleton troops.

As she traveled, she rehearsed the spiel meant to convince Lady Craven's officers to let her ally with them: "I'm Drift, from the Mushroom Island 6 griefers. We lost our base during that last tsunami. I heard about your cause and want to join up."

Frida knew she would have to perform a test to prove her trustworthiness. Her battalion supply chief, Jools, had equipped her with TNT and fire starter to booby-trap the enemy camp, but the explosives would also be believable griefer weapons. She'd just have to find the right moment to wield them, preferably not against civilians.

She sighed. Liberating villagers and safeguarding borders was not her career of choice. She had been born a survivalist, trained by skilled women to fend for herself in the jungle. Her goal was simply to live a good life, undisturbed by the dark forces of the world. In better days, she had done just that. But now that the mobs had been rallied and unified by sorcerers bent on conquering the free lands, that life was over . . . unless Frida and her compatriots could prevent or win an all-out war. *Better to be on the offensive than the defensive*, she thought, glad to have undertaken a solo mission to stir things up. Maybe she could put Battalion Zero in the win column this time around. Still, she'd have to confront her opponents first, deliberately making herself a target.

"I might as well call myself *Bull's-Eye*," she mumbled.

Basically asking to be attacked reminded her of climbing on a horse for the first time. She and her pals in Rob's cavalry unit had discovered that taming and riding wild beasts was easier said than done—but it was something Frida had always wanted to do. The ability to ride could certainly benefit a young woman making her way in the Overworld alone. Horses were fast, they could jump high, and—Frida had to admit—they were good company. She had never needed company before, but after riding with the battalion, she had grown used to the closeness.

As unfamiliar as her solitude seemed now, she was enjoying the feeling of freedom that came from surviving alone. A chicken tottered into view through the high plains grass, and Frida pulled out her iron sword and dispatched the bird, eating it immediately. She waited a moment to see whether the raw flesh would make her sick, but it didn't. Risks never bothered her when the chance of success was greater than or equal to that of harm. *This larger risk, though . . .*

. . . would be worth it, she had already decided. She repeated aloud the sentiment that Corporal Kim had once voiced: "The only acceptable Overworld is a free Overworld." Frida would have to leave that notion at the plains boundary, though, which she could make out across the dusky fields in the distance. There, Lady Craven's underlings would be waiting.

"I'm Drift . . ." she said again, as though to convince herself.

Soon, she approached the border where open grasslands met rocky foothills. At least she knew the odds of skeletons spawning there: 100 percent. She pulled out her bow and stuck an arrow in the back waistband of her pants. It wouldn't do to appear aggressive, but then again, a girl had to be ready to defend herself.

The suspense did not last long.

Th-oop! Thoo-thoo-thoo-ppp! An arrow landed at her feet, and then three more in a circle around her. They had flown from a dark thicket of spruce trees up ahead. "Do I have to be right all the time?" she muttered.

"Identify yourself, traveler!" came a nasal voice that Frida knew well.

Its owner knew her, too, but had not identified her—so perhaps the ploy was working already. Frida certainly didn't look like herself anymore.

"They call me Drift," she said to the unseen creature in the trees, just as she'd rehearsed. "I have business with the griefer boss, Lady Craven!"

A taunting laugh sailed her way. "But does she have business with you? I doubt it."

Already, Frida tired of talking with the cowardly griefer, Legs, who always hid behind any handy bodyguard. "Then come out where we can see each other, and I'll prove it to you."

"Prove it to this!" the stuffy voice demanded.

The next thing Frida knew, a cross-looking creeper broke out of the brush and ate up the distance between them. Frida didn't want to waste three arrows on this mobster right off the bat, so she stood her ground. The creeper's patchy green skin and hollow black eye sockets did not scare her off.

Before it could get within detonation range, Frida exchanged her bow for flint and steel from her inventory. *Ch-oom!* The next best thing to avoiding a creeper's explosion was to make one ignite.

"Is that the best you've got?" Frida called.

Out of the spruce tree shade stepped a squat griefer with a large nose and three skinny legs. "You know of our secret handshake," said Legs. "You may cross the boundary."

Luck! Blowing up creepers was how this bunch said hello. Simply by choosing the right weapon, Frida had gained valuable information. She moved forward, past the burned spot on the ground left by the exploding mobster. It was all she could do not to draw her sword on Legs, the scum who had threatened her friends and innocent villagers so many times in the past. But a little restraint now would give her access to many more of Lady Craven's minions.

Suddenly, baby zombies surrounded her, grabbing at her clothing and all but holding her hostage with their stench. Among the zombies, only the babies wouldn't burn up in the day's fading sunlight. Frida balled up her fists as the tiny monsters reached out and immobilized her. *Not the kind of restraint I had in mind*, she thought.

Capture was a necessary part of Frida's plan, so she played along with Legs.

"Please let me go! I'm a griefer, just like you. The last tsunami destroyed our island base and scattered our numbers."

"That may be," Legs said. "Why should we accept you?"

Frida struggled with the stinking baby zombies but let them hang on to her. "I've heard of your cause. I hate all those villagers, running around loose like they own the world. I want to join up with your operation and finish them off, once and for all."

Legs sized her up, then waved a hand at the zombies, who let her go. "This way," he said and led her into the gloom beneath the spruce trees.

Before Frida's eyes could focus, she heard the characteristic jittering and twanging of skeletons fiddling with their bowstrings. She tried not to flinch. Any weakness on her part might cause them to fall on her like a pack of undead dogs.

"Okay," said Legs. "We'll hear you out, stranger. Then decide whether you live or die." He tossed some spider string to another human—his face as craggy as the foothills—and motioned for him to tie Frida up. "Make it tight, Dingo! That way, she can't reach her inventory." The sharp-featured underling lashed Frida's wrists together and then panted as he went to work on her ankles. Drool fell from his slack lips onto Frida's bare skin, and she cringed. Somewhere behind her, the skeletons shifted their bones, waiting for a command.

Frida took a deep breath and launched into her made-up story. "MI 6 made a perfect retreat for our griefer ring after attacking villages. We'd get plenty of loot by burning out towns and then floating the stuff out to the island by boat."

"So, what's not to like?" Legs asked.

"Wasn't enough. The villagers would just rebuild, and we'd have to reattack. We wanted to see griefers control all of the Overworld riches, for good."

Dingo grunted.

Legs stroked his chin. "It does seem to be an endless task. But Lady Craven has a system now."

"I'm sure you can use another hand," Frida said. "So, here I am, ready to help take back the biomes from the peasants. The people with the most power *should* rule them."

Legs rewarded her solidarity by releasing her. "We need someone like you to oversee the zombies on the western boundary. You're on probation, Drift. Handle your first assignment, and we might move you up to skeleton duty." He tossed her a medallion that would identify her as one of them—a gold pendant in the shape of the initials *LC*—which she hung around her neck.

The job entailed steering the enchanted adult and baby zombies to the border at nightfall, where they could attack unsuspecting tourists, and then back to a cavern beyond the spruce trees in the morning. It seemed easy enough, but organizing the wayward zombies was like herding cats. Legs had Dingo show

Frida the ropes and supervise her work until she got the hang of it.

A few days later, they left her to the task and went to burn a village on the other side of the hills, where Lady Craven was waiting. "Don't try anything! Somebody will be watching you. Do your job, Drift, and we'll save you some plunder!" Legs called merrily over his shoulder.

This was the opportunity Frida had anticipated.

That night, she followed her zombie pack to the plains boundary, where she had hidden most of her inventory before meeting the griefers. The enchantment kept the mobs from considering her a threat, so she had no trouble leading them into a blind canyon. She rolled a large boulder in front of its narrow opening and left the zombies there, moaning, where no one could hear them. Then she retrieved her spare supplies and set about rigging trip wires and placing TNT charges by the light of the moon.

After completing the task, she prepared to head for the rendezvous point to wait till daybreak and signal her battalion. Just then, though, an unfamiliar griefer in a baseball cap skirted the cliffside, his gang medallion swinging like a pendulum. Seeing him coming around the rock wall that hid her zombies from view, Frida hurried toward him, hoping he wouldn't hear the intermittent groans.

"Ahoy!" she called. "What's up?"

"Legs sent me," the thin, long-armed griefer said, his knuckles nearly dragging on the ground. "I'm supposed to stay hidden and keep an eye on—" He realized his mistake. "Oh, darn! I knew I'd get that wrong!"

"Nothing to see here," Frida said mildly, turning sideways and pulling her sword. "Except this!" She whirled and sliced him clean through his middle. His saucer eyes rolled as his top half hit the ground. Then his legs upended themselves like toppled bowling pins. "Go spawn somewhere else," Frida growled, and ran off up the hill.

*

Once at the appointed coordinates, she couldn't wait to get out of her costume and false skin. While Frida was busy changing, a pack of zombies spawned nearby.

"*Uuuuhh, ooohhh . . .*" they moaned like a disorganized choir.

She noticed them stumbling in circles, ignoring her. When she removed the medallion that Legs had given her, however, they instantly menaced her. She put the pendant back on. They stopped. Again, she took it off, and they targeted her once more.

"That's it." She grinned and replaced the chain around her neck. It appeared to work as a repellant, which would spare her dwindling inventory of ammunition or energy in a fight. *Amazing!* This was better than a splash potion.

Frida felt secure enough to let herself doze against a spruce tree.

The sun came up, and there was nothing left to do but bide her time until its rays cleared the opposite ridgeline and hit the ground at her feet. Frida could remain motionless for hours. She used the time to kick around a few ideas. One was finding a way to get to her family reunion this time around. She'd missed the last few by dying and respawning in inconvenient places. It was high time she saw her female relatives. She might even be able to enlist them in helping save the Overworld. If she could talk Rob into filling her vanguard position with a substitute for a while, she'd be able to do it.

Rob . . . Roberto, the captain of Battalion Zero, was the other main subject of her thoughts lately. Rob had been a cowboy before spawning in the Overworld and putting together a mounted unit. He and Frida had met when he literally fell into her world from an airplane. She'd helped him survive his first days here as he fumbled about, completely unprepared for handling hostile mobs and boundary disputes. But, somehow, the tables had turned, and Frida had watched the castaway cowboy put his smarts to use as a cavalry captain, flowering as an effective leader right before her eyes.

There was something incredibly attractive about that. She wasn't the only one who'd noticed. Frida knew that Rob had feelings for Stormie and Kim, the other women in their group. Fortunately—and unfortunately—the straight-arrow captain knew better than to romance any of his troops. He kept his sights firmly set on defending Overworld boundaries from tyrants and their hostile mobs.

As the sun dappled the ground just outside the tree line, Frida realized she'd been lost in her thoughts too long.

She scrambled to her feet and fished in her inventory for a piece of glass. She used it to catch the sunlight and reflect it across the hillside, flashing the code Jools had devised. It showed where Frida had placed the trip wires and let the battalion know she was safe.

Frida could only hope that her friends had arrived and seen her message. Then, once again, she hunkered down to wait until darkness fell.

*

With the dusk came the sound of human voices to the west. Frida got to her feet and squinted. She could hear whooping but could not see anyone approaching. She tensed; the plan was unfolding just as Jools had laid it out. The villagers they'd enlisted as ground troops were announcing their presence to arouse the griefers' interest and to send their mobs through the booby trap. It was time for Frida to make her getaway.

A cacophony of moans filled the air as the griefers' zombie reinforcements were loosed in the villagers' direction. Their cries reverberated off the cliffs and canyons of the extreme hills: "Uuuuh-*uh-uh-uh* . . . oooh-*oh-oh-oh* . . . !"

To Frida's intense relief, she spied her old friend and sometime adversary, Turner, riding his gray quarter horse, Duff, toward her at a rapid pace. And he was leading her black pony, Ocelot. How glad she was to have learned to ride.

She shouted to Turner, who came close and threw her Ocelot's reins.

"I've got your armor, Frida, but we'd best get out of here first!" said the company's sergeant at arms. He was a mercenary by trade but a soldier by necessity. Anyone who wanted to stay free in the Overworld had to contribute to the war effort against Lady Craven.

Frida leapt from the ground onto Ocelot's saddle as though she'd been doing it her whole life. She followed Turner and Duff, galloping like the wind, to rejoin her battalion. She'd never been so happy to leave her solo status behind.

CHAPTER 2

ONE DAY LATER

FRIDA LED OCELOT THROUGH THE NETHER portal and joined the rest of her battalion on the surface. She turned the pony in a circle, taking in the snowy blocks that formed low terraces all around them. Above, the sky was a washed-out blue, broken by a few square clouds. The same color scheme lay beneath their feet, in a frozen river dotted with ice cubes. *Out of the frying pan and into the fire*, she thought.

"Nice place for a picnic," said Turner, reminding his friends that their hunger status was critical. The mercenary, himself, was so thin that his many tattoos had collapsed into meaningless squiggles.

The horses' health was iffy, too. Although the animals and soldiers had fled from Lady Craven's army, without some sustenance, they wouldn't last much longer. Unless they wanted to eat snow, they'd have to seek out a food source.

"Hey, team! I see some vegetation off that way," Quartermaster Jools said, mounting his tall, cream-colored horse, Beckett. In his weakened state, Jools was a good three shades paler than the palomino, and his rumpled tweed jacket hung on him like an empty sock. "Follow us."

Frida—appearing more wiry than ever—got up on Ocelot and fell in next to Turner on Duff and the black and white paint horse they were leading. Kim, dressed in her customary riding clothes and boots, sprang onto Nightwind. Her naturally pink skin belied her poor health, but her tiny form had shrunk with hunger. The experienced rider seemed ill-matched with the big bay stallion that their friend and adviser, Colonel M, had bequeathed to her. Rob, the battalion's captain, remained on the ground, leading his black horse, which was limping.

"Saber's all in," Rob said, so Turner gave him the spare horse, Armor, to ride, and he ponied Saber alongside. They trailed behind the others, an unusually gaunt Rob gawking at the surroundings. He had arrived in this version of the Overworld not so long ago and could still be considered a newbie. Hailing from the high desert in his world, he had never seen a stretch of ice plains before, nor strolled across a frozen river.

Frida reined Ocelot in and waited for Rob to catch up. Ever since she'd trapped him on his first day in the jungle, she had felt it her duty to teach him how to survive. He couldn't have stumbled across a better tutor. "Hang in there, Captain," Frida encouraged him. "We're bound to find something to eat soon."

"Or someone to trade with," Kim added.

Their inventories had been replenished with diamonds, gold, and other bankable ores by Colonel M, but the old ghost could not offer them any food. He had escorted them swiftly from portal to portal in his native Nether, moving them out of Lady Craven's range, but temporarily stranding them here in the desolate snowy plains on the surface. They'd have to keep moving if they wanted to save themselves.

Battalion Zero's ammunition was spent, and their weapons were damaged. Worst of all, they'd lost Artilleryman Stormie. They couldn't do anything about that, but at least it was morning, and they had the day to travel unbothered by hostile mobs to seek food.

Frida's stomach grumbled. She had been raised to fend for herself and would've had no trouble getting by on her own. *Groups complicate everything*, she thought. They required more food, more resources, and more protection just to stay in the game. She said as much to Rob, who had unwittingly been thrust into the role of troop leader—a position as unnatural to him as it was to her. He'd told her that in his old life, he had often ridden fences for days on end seeing no one but his horse, his dog, and a few stray cows. Maybe that was why Frida felt so close to him.

"Hey, sugarcane!" Jools called, as they moved into a small patch of reeds.

The limited supply proved Frida's point that groups were troublesome. There was enough cane to craft sugar for the horses, but not enough to prevent the troopers from starving. While she might share food with her comrades, she resolved to keep her magical griefer medallion a secret unless she absolutely had to use it.

"Chins up, Bat Zero!" Kim said with forced cheer. "Pepping up the horses will get us where we're going faster."

"Wherever that is," Frida mumbled. She could always determine a course for herself, but, until recently, she had left company movement to Rob and Stormie. Without the expert adventurer and her map, though, their destination was less than certain.

Rob was trying to maintain his command, no matter how difficult it had become. He summoned Frida after Ocelot had munched her small ration of sugar cubes. "Vanguard, ride out and see if you can spot the village that Colonel M mentioned."

The First War veteran had sent them through the nearest escape portal, assuring them that they could reach an ice plains village called Spike City by nightfall if they hurried. Frida rode off to scout ahead, giving the battalion a good view of Ocelot's brown-spotted rump as the pony galloped toward the horizon.

Horse and rider hopped up and down the low snow terraces, soon coming upon a small thicket of trees. Among the dark spruce rose a couple of oaks. Frida paused long enough to stand in the saddle and whack down an armload of apples. She crammed one in her mouth, gave one to Ocelot, and saved the rest for her friends. A wry smile crossed her green lips as she trotted away again. *What would Mami have to say about this?* Sharing would have been unthinkable in her old life, where survival of the fittest demanded an unflinchingly selfish attitude.

Reaching a small six-block rise, Frida urged her horse upward to view the landscape. Off to the southwest, Frida could see the carpet of snow give way to higher-elevation forest. She noted its potential for a base hideout. Sure enough, off to the north, a facade rose from the plains in the distance—a sizable collection of ice spike formations that the colonel said had been settled by villagers. The wiry vanguard sighed with relief and wheeled her horse around to carry the good news back to the banished lot of soldiers.

*

Rob nodded through a mouthful of apple as Frida gave him her full report. "Thanks, Frida. That terrain intel gives me an idea. Battalion," he announced, "we'll split into two squadrons. Jools, Kim—you'll ride south with me to build shelter. Frida and Turner will cash in some diamonds for food in the village and join us ASAP. Oh, and see what you two can dredge up in the way of work. We're going to need some serious loot to fund our next campaign."

The two squads separated. Frida and Turner directed their own mounts northward. The sugar and apples had restored energy levels sufficiently to enable fast transport. They soon reached the outskirts of the largest city that either of the survivalists had ever visited.

Packed ice covered the ground and shot upward in tower formations, which enterprising players had hollowed out and made habitable. Frida felt as spellbound as her newbie captain would have been at the sight of the sparkling condominiums lining the ice pathway. Torches burned brightly on the wayside, giving the town a holiday atmosphere.

In reality, though, life in Spike City was no party. Far from its nearest neighbors, this settlement was its own survival island, and the population reflected that rugged state. Villagers in threadbare aprons bustled to and fro with their wares. Coarse-looking farmers tended heated and covered garden strips. Ragged children engaged the local snow golem in a harmless snowball fight.

Frida and Turner rode up the main street until they came to a butcher shop. "I'll hold the horses, Meat," Frida said, using her pet name for her old friend. "You go get us some steaks."

"Meat's my middle name," he said amiably, leaving Duff behind.

She kept her ears open while she waited. Eavesdropping was a skill that all of her female family members were required to hone. Frida soon overheard a priest chatting with a villager about a supply train that was scheduled to arrive in a few days.

"It's bringing a gem shipment down from the extreme hills," the long-haired cleric in the frayed purple robe said. "Coming this direction, the griefers won't find out about it."

The leather worker dressed in a dirty white apron shrugged. "But the syndicate will. We'll be lucky to get a pile of gravel by the time they're through with it."

They grumbled a bit more, and the tradesman walked off.

"Say, Padre," Frida said before the priest could also disappear. "It sounds as though you folks could use some muscle to secure your payday."

The cleric acknowledged the girl with a tip of his shaggy head. "It's an ongoing problem, but there's always a way to score if you hire the right people."

Frida narrowed her eyes. "Are you saying there's bodyguarding work available?"

The cleric smiled, revealing a few rotten teeth, but there was no humor in his expression. "If folks are willing to risk their lives for it."

"Is there any other way to work?" she asked.

"Look, let's talk about this somewhere more . . . private." He glanced over his shoulder.

Turner walked toward them, chewing on something. The meal had restored his normal stature: big, beefy, and almost completely covered with skin art representing the Overworld biomes. His version of Friday casual—ripped T-shirt, cargo pants, and combat boots—stood out among the frocked villagers.

"Turner, the padre here has some news for us," Frida said. "What's your name, by the way?"

"*Padre* will do," he said. "Come along."

As he turned to usher them down the street, Frida noticed a small marking on the back of his neck when his hair momentarily shifted—a tattoo of an apple with an arrow in it. Just like the one she had.

She froze for an instant, then followed, pretending not to notice. "Whatcha eating, Meat?" she asked Turner, handing him Duff's reins and trying to distract him so he wouldn't spot the familiar tattoo. Turner, himself, was so heavily decorated that one tat might not make an impression.

Turner mumbled an incomprehensible reply and handed Frida some beef jerky from his new supply. They turned down a side street, after the padre who led them through a door, and inside a spike dwelling set with stained-glass windows. The entryway was decorated with a font that dripped water from an ice block set over a blue beacon. It looked to be the only thing nearby not made of packed ice.

"You can bring your horses right on in," the padre said. "There's plenty of room."

Indeed, the ice chapel was meant for a large congregation, but sat empty right now . . . save for one soul who awaited the priest's return. The young woman in short shorts and a black crop top stood on the other side of the wide room with her back to the door, a long, wavy, black ponytail cascading over one shoulder. She turned to face the visitors, and surprise crossed her dusky face.

Frida and Turner volleyed the disbelief right back at her.

"*Stormie?*" Frida exclaimed.

The woman squealed in answer and rushed forward, startling the horses and the priest. She opened her arms and crushed Frida and Turner in a group hug.

"*Ow!*" Turner complained, obviously more pleased than harmed.

"Did you spawn here?" Frida asked.

"I brought her here," the padre said, annoyed that he'd been left out of the conversation. "You people know each other? She's looking for work, too." He regarded the trio. "I think you'd better tell me who you are. *Now.*"

Turner opened his mouth, but Frida cut him off before he could say a word. "Okay, Padre." She sent Stormie a meaningful stare. "We're a mercenary collective, trying to stay afloat while we build up our herd of horses. You've met Stormie, here, the well-known adventurer. Turner's a solid hand with weapons, and I'm a survivalist by trade. We can team up to provide whatever protection your people need."

"And who are you?"

"Me?" Frida paused. "I'm your sister."

*

The padre's name was Rafe—short for Rafael, one of Frida's clan who had been sent away at age eight to be raised by villagers.

He and Frida compared neck artwork.

"Sweet!" admired Turner.

"What's the apple stand for?" Stormie asked.

"It's our family crest," Frida replied. "We come from jungle country, thick with apple-bearing oaks."

"And the arrow . . . ?"

"Stands for this!" Rafe cried, springing at Frida and taking her down. They tussled, rolling on the packed-ice floor, each trying to pin the other.

Finally, Turner broke up the sparring match. "Hey! Hey! C'mon, you appleseeds. We get it. You like to fight." He grinned and elbowed Stormie. "Separated at birth, huh? Two peas in a pod."

When they parted, Rafe explained that they'd play-fought as kids. He knew that Frida would have gone on to learn the advanced technical skills that all the women warriors in their family were trained in. He'd entered the church and found it an ideal way to remain outside the limits of the law. "Where there's good, there's bound to be evil," he explained. "Being a priest is the best way to make deals with the dark side."

Turner grunted. "And that's always where the money is."

"Sad but true," Rafe agreed.

One thing still bothered Frida about her long-lost brother: boys in the family weren't tattooed as the girls were when they'd completed their training and set off on their own. But she wouldn't ask about it now. Mark or no mark, he was clearly one of her clan, and he appeared to be just what the battalion needed.

Frida indicated to her friends that they could trust him well enough, so they gave him the bare details of their mission and their somewhat desperate circumstances.

"I don't know about saving the Overworld," Rafe said. "I'm not really a joiner. That's why I came out here. Spike City is more an outpost than a village. Folks come here after being thrown out or chased away from more respectable places. Mostly, they just want to be left alone."

"But it seems so . . . upscale," Stormie remarked.

"Well, builders have a lot of time on their hands and plenty of stolen goods to buy cheap."

"Sounds like my kinda town," Turner said, rubbing his hands together.

"Don't get any retirement ideas, Meat," Frida scolded. "We've got a job to do first."

She assured her brother that their crew would be interested in any risky employment opportunities with decent payoff to fund their crusade. He said he'd talk to his people.

"We've got to go, Rafe. We'll be in touch."

The brother and sister pounded fists, and the three reunited friends took their leave, marveling at their good luck. The turn of events had been amazing, even by extremely rare world probability standards.

*

"But how did you get here?" Frida asked Stormie as they rode southward, away from the village. Turner had pulled Stormie up to ride behind Duff's saddle.

"Well, I just followed the plan we'd agreed on back at Bryce Mesa for if we died and respawned. Remember?"

Turner scratched his head. "That was one losing battle and two portals ago," he pointed out.

"I was supposed to get to the Nether and wait for y'all at the safe house," Stormie said. "I probably showed up there before the last skeleton's arrow hit your butt."

Frida laughed. "Once we entered the Nether, we didn't slow down until Colonel M sent us back out onto the ice plains. He made sure the griefers couldn't follow us."

"When nobody showed up," Stormie said, "I went to the colonel's fortress. He told me you'd eventually surface in the city. Funny that we were both drawn to your brother, though."

"No mistake, there." Frida nodded at Turner. "We both know how to find a good con man."

"Amen to that, sisters," he declared proudly.

They journeyed to the coordinates that the two squadrons had agreed on as a meeting point. When they arrived, though, they found an empty stone enclosure and a note: *Gone horse hunting.*

Turner drifted off to explore the area, leaving the two women in the hut to catch up on the details of Frida's secret mission.

*

". . . and that's where you came in," Frida said to Stormie, who sat cross-legged next to her in the stone shelter. The whole incident Frida had just recounted had been merely a prelude to their current predicament. That battle had been lost—and lost big. Like it or not, Battalion Zero was on the run.

"That's also where I went out," Stormie replied, referring to her untimely death at the hands of griefer skelemobs.

"Yeah, but you came back to fight with us another day." Frida held out two palms.

Stormie slapped them. "I told you so, girl."

"Glad to have you back," Frida said.

"Glad to be back. So, besides wangling jobs and building up our inventories, what's the plan?"

The battalion had been forced to flee to a rough patch in the Overworld—one that made survival, let alone looting, a trial. Resources were scarce and settlements few and far between in the cold and snowy biomes. It had become clear that Rob and company would have to bend a few of society's rules in order to reequip themselves to do battle.

"The captain thought it would be a good idea to pick up some legit travelers and act as guides. That'll give us a chance to keep on the move and look honest while we turn some jobs into gems."

"The kind of jobs Rafe was talking about could get us in hot water," Stormie said.

"And those are the jobs that pay, as he was saying. So, first we needed to get food and supplies. Me and Turner handled that. The others built this shelter, and I imagine they've already got a line on some extra horses. We'll need them to shepherd tourists around."

"Awesome," Stormie said. "I can't wait to see ever'body. How *is* the captain?"

Frida hesitated. She hadn't shared her thoughts about Rob with Stormie, and there was no point in doing so now. "He's fine." Frida heard hoof beats in the distance and put up a finger. "Listen. They're coming. He can tell you how he's doing himself."

They got to their feet and went outside to greet the others. The sound of hooves grew louder, and a cluster of horses could be seen through the trees.

Frida frowned. "They're moving awfully fast," she murmured.

"I'll say!"

On rushed a trio of loose horses, with Rob, Kim, and Jools pushing them before Armor, Nightwind, and Beckett at a flat-out run. Frida had never seen placid Beckett gallop so fast.

Stormie's welcoming smile faded as Rob called out, "Take shelter! Get inside!"

Stormie and Frida waited just long enough to watch the three riders run the other horses into a hole in the ground that served as a makeshift corral, where the injured Saber was waiting. Jumping off, Rob and company pushed their own mounts in. Then everybody dove for the stone hut.

The squadron's shock at seeing their fallen comrade again had to take a backseat to the more pressing crisis. "Where's Turner?" Rob shouted. "I think we're in for a fight."

Turner's absence would not be appreciated.

"How'd you get those horses?" Frida asked.

"How do you think!" Rob snapped. "We stole 'em."

CHAPTER 3

JOOLS OPENED A CHEST THAT SAT IN A CORNER OF the hut and supplied everyone with wooden axes. "These were all we had the time and materials to craft," he said, apologizing.

"Battle stations!" Rob cried. "We've got to safeguard the horses."

Rob, Jools, Kim, Frida, and Stormie spilled back out the door just as a posse of three riders on two horses and a mule clattered up to the corral.

"Shove off! You're outnumbered." Rob brandished his axe at the squadron's pursuers. The other battalion members crowded around him.

The posse's leader pushed a leather cap back on her forehead and snorted. "Youse outgunned!" she said, patting her modified crossbow and nodding toward her equally armed cohorts. "Let them hosses go. We come by 'em fair and square." She frowned. "Well, square, anyhow."

"We saw you rustle those mounts from that farmer!" Kim shouted, accusing the surly woman.

"They was . . . payment!"

"Payment for what? A shipment of ugly?" Jools taunted.

"Why I oughtta—" The woman drew her crossbow.

Thwank! A stone axe sailed from behind and knocked the crossbow out of her hand. The other two riders fumbled for their weapons.

"Drop 'em!" Turner called, stepping from behind a tree. When the mounted men didn't comply fast enough, Turner grasped the axe he was carrying at either end and knocked one man to the left and the other to the right, out of their saddles and onto the ground. The mule let out a distinctive bray.

Stormie rushed forward and scooped up the crossbows. Rob retrieved the mule by its bridle and motioned to the other horse. "Mount up and light out!" he ordered the two men on the ground.

They scrambled to their feet and onto the remaining animal, whirling to retreat along with their leader. The troopers of Battalion Zero pelted them with dirt clods.

"We'll be back!" yelled the leather-clad woman. "Nobody gets the better of Precious McGee!"

Frida watched them ride off. "Looks like you made some new friends while we were gone, Captain."

Rob shrugged.

"Lucky I had time to craft this." Turner bent down and pulled his stone axe out of the earth, where it had landed blade first. "You mighta warned us," he groused.

"Yeah, well, things don't always go according to plan," said the cowboy-turned-cavalry commander. He certainly looked the part of the wrangler in his leather riding chaps, vest, and Western-style shirt. "I'm going by one rule right now: don't take from honest villagers."

"But taking from those who *take* from the villagers is acceptable," Jools clarified with only a hint of irony.

Once the horses were secured and everyone had calmed down, they could turn their attention to celebrating the reunion with Stormie. Kim hugged her. Jools saluted. Rob coughed and backed off a pace when she tried to embrace him. "Nice to see you, Artilleryman," he said.

As they caught up with Stormie on what had happened since the Battle of Zombie Hill, Turner handed out some pickaxes he'd crafted. They all reentered the stone hut and worked at widening the back wall, which was part of a natural cave. The horses would need to come inside once it got dark out, to protect them from any hostile predators . . . including human ones.

Frida had to admit that she enjoyed being with her friends, chatting and plotting and acting with a common purpose once more. They used some of the coal that Colonel M had given them and wood that Turner had felled to craft torches to illuminate the cavern. Kim lit the furnace and cooked some beef to snack on. Jools collected useful cobblestone and ore that they chipped away, and, just like that, the battalion was once more on solid footing. Although Frida had often faced starvation, she was especially relieved to have avoided it now that the gang was all together again. Death and respawning was another pesky threat that came with running in groups. They had been incredibly lucky to meet up with Stormie again. They could have become separated forever.

The Overworld traveler's good fortune, however, had not been complete. Stormie had been unable to reclaim the inventory she'd dropped back in the extreme hills. The loss of her map would be felt the most keenly.

"Reckon I'll just start over," she said when Frida brought up the subject. "Terrain intelligence is always worth money, especially out on the fringes."

Rob noted that they'd need gems to repay the wheat farmer for his animals and for a steady supply of hay. "What've you got left after your trip to the grocery store, Sergeant Major?" he asked Turner.

Their ore stash would only pay for one more food run or some small weaponry trades. They'd hit a small pocket of iron that could be used to craft a few helmets or chest plates but not enough to armor the whole battalion.

"We'll divide into squadrons for the risky stuff, then," Rob said. "Turner, you'll ride with Frida and Stormie, in charge of B Squadron. Kim will head A Squadron, subject to my orders. We'll trade off, one unit acting as tour guides, and the other working at such jobs as we come by."

"We've got a line on employment," Frida reported. "Where are we going to find these tourists to act as cover?"

Rob grinned. "That's your first official duty, B Squadron. As soon as we're shored up here in camp, we'll visit Spike City to fulfill both missions. You're to be commended for your advance work, Vanguard."

Frida was touched that Rob had recognized her in front of the troops. She knew her skills made her a valuable member of the team. But that also might make it difficult to secure a leave of absence to attend her family gathering.

Instinctively, her hand went to the back of her neck, and she rubbed her tattoo. She wondered how her mother, sisters, and aunts were surviving in the increasingly dangerous Overworld. Perhaps they were staying away from the biome boundaries.

That didn't make them free, though, and Frida had vowed to battle the griefer army until they were free once more. *I could really use some advice from old Xanto*, she thought grimly. She decided that, one way or another, she would be at her family's survivalist rally.

*

The reunited friends lost track of the hour. By the time they had finally enlarged their structure to accommodate the livestock, dusk had fallen. They went outside together, Turner's squadron armed to protect Kim's unit, as they led the animals into the shelter. The move proved fortunate.

A mob of zombies tottered out of the trees and spied them. *"Uuuuhh . . . ooohhh!"* The threatening groans turned to moans of defeat at the hands of Turner and Stormie, who had to whack at the monsters over and over for their wooden swords to do damage. Frida hung back, escaping the worst of the smell as she watched for other hostiles. She darted forward to pick up what the zombies dropped when they were neutralized. Carrots, potatoes, rotten flesh, and some used chainmail armor went into the communal war chest, while she kept the knowledge of her mob-repellant pendant to herself.

After putting their mounts in the fortified cave, Rob, Jools, and Horse Master Kim made a second trip to collect the new horses and mule.

But Frida sighted another green-skinned intruder. "Creeper coming! Run, gang!" she called. Sticks and swords would do them no good against the exploding creature. She calculated the distance between them and the creeper, acting as a decoy as long as she could stay out of range. Then she turned tail and escaped to the cave entrance, just as the mobster blew up on the edge of the corral.

"Well, now we've got a bigger horse pen," she quipped, slipping inside after the others and slamming the wooden door shut.

They used the evening to mine and make plans. No one had a bed to sleep in, anyway.

"Maybe that farmer has some sheep," Kim said.

"Suppose we die before getting any wool to make beds," Jools remarked. "What will our rendezvous position be upon respawn?"

Frida told everyone about her brother's church in the big village. "Rafe will take us in," she said. "And a priest is good cover for any . . . undercover activities that might cause our deaths."

"Good point," Rob agreed. "If you die and respawn, we'll meet up at the church in Spike City. Use the Nether if you need to cross boundaries to get there. Colonel M said he'd be on the lookout for us."

Frida trusted the First War veteran implicitly, which was more than she could say for her brother. But she didn't mention her misgivings to the rest of the battalion. She would sort Rafe out soon enough. In the meantime, their few remaining gems would be enough to buy his hospitality, if need be.

"We'll go see him tomorrow," Frida said, offering to introduce Rob to the cleric to negotiate their first job. Meanwhile, she and Stormie would sign up their first tourists. Turner would be nearby, in case there was any trouble.

"So, who should we be looking for, Captain?" Stormie asked.

"Anyone who's *not* trouble," Rob said. "We want folks who can pay, number one, and skilled travelers, number two. Find people who can do what we don't have time for—mining, building, crafting. . . ."

"Plenty of them in that city," Turner noted.

"Try and be selective," Jools said. "Avoid the low types." He eyed Turner. "We've got one of those already."

"Enough, you two," Rob said. "That's why I'm putting Frida on the job. She'll vet any applicants for soundness. It'd be nice to sign up a librarian or someone with legitimate credentials, to make us appear law abiding."

Stormie nodded. "Someone reputable, then."

"However foreign that might be to us," Jools murmured, and ducked as Turner threw a potato at him.

*

They set out for the city the next day, all except Kim, who stayed behind to keep tabs on the new horses and mule. "Bring me back a present!" she called.

Once in town, Frida left Rob and Jools to speak with Rafe about work, and Turner to make trades, while she and Stormie advertised their travel service. They set up a station at the village well, which would get all kinds of foot traffic, and began calling out to passersby.

"Seasoned guides, reasonable rates!" barked Stormie.

"Fast horses, expert escorts," cried Frida.

A few people expressed curiosity in riding with their group, but they weren't the type the captain had in mind. "I think you'd be happier with another guide," Frida said to a woman who had nothing to trade and, again, to a little boy who appeared to be running away from home.

At last, a couple of players made the grade—a teenage brother-and-sister pair who were exploring the Overworld, searching for a place to settle down and start a new life. The girl was a miner and the boy, a builder. They might have spawned somewhere near Jools's starting point, as they had a similar translucent skin and light hair coloring. Their practical safari-style clothing and comfortable slip-on shoes were appropriate for long-term travel.

"Names?" Frida demanded.

"I'm De Vries," replied the young man in a lilting voice, "and this is my sister, Crash." He offered three emeralds as a down payment. Crash threw in a diamond pickaxe.

"Any objections to riding with an armed battalion? Our first loyalty is to our cause of defending the Overworld; your wishes come second."

Not only did the two not object, they seemed quite interested in Battalion Zero's campaign against Lady Craven and her griefers. They passed Frida's white-hot scrutiny and went off to buy supplies.

She and Stormie kept at it and got a few more serious inquiries from prospects that Frida ultimately deemed incompatible with their mission.

Then an older gentleman walking by responded to Stormie's pitch. His hair was white with gray around the edges, and his skin was a rich brown. He wore a tailored cloak and carried a briefcase. "I'm looking to make a circuit with a reliable outfit," he said.

"Can you pay up front?" Frida asked, scanning his face for any hint of falseness.

"Of course."

"Destination?"

"Unknown. That is, I haven't decided yet."

"What have you got to trade?" Stormie pressed.

He handed her two emeralds and fished in his briefcase. "I don't know if you can use them or not, but I do have these." He handed her a book and a ring. "I won't be needing them anymore."

"*Principles of Law*," she read. "And a United Biomes of the Overworld ring. You a judge?"

"Was," he acknowledged. "I'm pursuing a new career."

"Anybody pursuing you?"

"Not that I know of." He smiled.

A shadow fell on him from behind. "Is this fella bothering you?" Turner asked gruffly.

Frida rose. "Not at all. In fact, he appears to be the soul of reason."

"Thank you, young lady," the judge said. "Now, when do we depart?"

"In some kind of hurry?" Turner probed.

The man studied Turner's weathered face and the colorful tattoos on the rest of his exposed skin. "*Tempus fugit*, son."

"Well, I don't know what that means, but the sun's going down already. Time sure flies when you're having fun."

They relayed the battalion mission and their rules, then agreed to meet Judge Tome, as he said his name was, and the other tourists at the well after sunup the next day. Then the troopers of B Squadron made their way to the chapel to see how their counterparts had fared.

"All set!" Rob said, slapping his thighs. "Rafe, here, has hooked us up with a guy named Bluedog who acts as a moneylender around these parts."

"Collection job?" Turner asked.

"Nope."

"Too bad. I'm good at persuading deadbeats to pay their bills." He flexed both biceps, causing his ink drawings of the mesa and desert biomes to ripple.

The purple-robed cleric stepped in to explain. "It's the supply train job I was telling you about. All you have to do to get your cut is ride along behind it as it comes down the mountain, yonder."

"Sounds simple enough," Stormie said.

"Yeah, but what'll be behind us?" Frida asked.

Rafe looked away. "Well, now. That's what you get paid to find out, isn't it?"

The troops were pumped about the prospects of work and income from the tourist business. "Playing travel guide'll give me a chance to work on my map," Stormie said as they headed back down the main packed-ice street on horseback.

"Playing bodyguard'll give me a chance to work on my wallet," Turner countered.

"*Our* wallet," Rob reminded him. "We *share* the inventory."

"Well, I hope there's something left over for the sergeant at arms," Turner grumbled. "Poor guy's gotta do all the hard work—bodyguarding, weapons crafting, and playing squadron babysitter. . . ."

Stormie and Frida glared at him. "*We're* the ones that got you paying jobs," Frida said.

"Yeah, Meat," Stormie goaded him. "Tough girls with pretty faces'll get more notice than just another killer-for-hire any day." She smiled sweetly. "In fact, I think you should buy us some flowers for setting you up with paid work."

Frida nodded at the town's farm stand, where colorful bouquets were for sale. "And while you're at it, buy a bunch for Kim. We promised to bring her a present."

CHAPTER 4

YEARS EARLIER

YOUNG FRIDA CREPT THROUGH THE JUNGLE, ALL senses on alert. Someone was following her, and learning whether he, she, or it was friend or foe could spell the difference between life and death. She turned left at a fork in the path, went a ways, and set a trip wire made of spider string. Then she doubled back through the underbrush, taking the path to the right this time. She tied a sapling to her waist and let it drag on the ground behind her, erasing her footprints as she moved on. If she didn't shake her shadower, she could kiss her freedom ceremony good-bye.

Everything she had done in her life had prepared her for this moment. Learning to track, forage, and camouflage herself . . . spending nights alone, with no shelter and few weapons . . . mastering trap setting and trickery to foil enemies. . . . Every skill had the same purpose—to allow her to survive on her own.

When she'd gone far enough to hide her whereabouts, she fell back again to the fork in the path and listened. Eyeing the ground, she saw two sets of footprints. Whoever was out there had followed her false tracks. Now she could become the hunter instead of the prey.

She crept ever so softly forward. A few moments passed, and she anticipated the sound of a body falling over her trip wire. Instead, she heard a *click* and froze. She'd stepped on a disguised pressure plate. Game over.

"You died!" came a female voice through the trees, echoed by several more.

The orchestrators ventured into the open and surrounded Frida, one of them reaching down to deactivate the plate, which could have powered any number of deadly devices to achieve her end.

Everything went foggy. Now Frida heard giggles and felt slender hands lifting her limp body off the harmless platform. *What's this? I failed miserably, and no one is calling me on it?*

"I'm so sorry," she murmured, but the other girls and women ignored her anguish.

"Congratulations, daughter," Frida's mother said, patting her shoulder. Gisel shared the smooth, olive-green skin and shiny, dark hair of her offspring. They looked like a mirror image when they kissed. "You have earned your freedom, little one."

"I . . . did?" Frida had been so intent on the exercise that she now found it hard to relax her taut muscles. As the sweat dried and her vision cleared, she tried to understand what her mother was saying. "But . . . you caught me. How could I have passed the test?"

Some of the others giggled again, and an elderly woman pushed through the crowd to speak with Frida. "Every girl in our clan passes the test," she said. "Just by staying alive to age fourteen."

"Did—did you do it, too, Xanto?"

The sage, whose shiny, dark hair nearly touched the ground, nodded. "And, although you fell short of perfection just now, you have passed where I was at your age."

That seemed impossible. The length of Xanto's hair indicated that she had already lived without respawning for longer than anyone else in the clan. "How so?" Frida asked.

"I never left the jungle." She pushed aside some well-placed leaves to indicate the jungle edge boundary. "You just did."

Frida received her apple tattoo, a small bundle of supplies, and a chaperone party to guide her to her new coordinates. There, she was freed from the protection of her family to make her way through the Overworld as she wished. She would only see them again periodically, when invited to the secret family rallies where they would connect, share wisdom and stories, and, finally, reassert their independence.

She would never forget that first step she took away from her people—and she wanted nothing more than to live until they next met.

*

That feeling washed over Frida now, as she made ready to hit the trail with her cavalry mates. Throwing in with this group went against all of her mother's teachings, all of Xanto's wisdom, and all of her own personal experience. But she recalled the assaults she'd suffered at the hands of Dr. Dirt, Lady Craven, and their griefer gang and sloughed off the guilt. As Jools had once said, if they didn't take a stand to save the Overworld from their domination now, there might not be a next time to try. Pulling a few jobs would help the battalion recover from their setback on Zombie Hill and allow them to live to fight another day.

Frida helped Kim ready the horses for travel, tossing them hay, checking their feet, and grooming them a bit to cozy them to the idea of carrying riders. Kim had evaluated and ridden the new animals and pronounced three of them up to the task. She would match them according to temperament and experience with those who had signed on to make the trip around the cold and snowy biomes. She deemed the short, stocky buckskin too rough for long-distance travel but ideal as a packhorse.

Frida wouldn't trade Ocelot on a bet, but she liked the new mare and stallion, a couple of thoroughbred crosses that Kim said could run and jump a derby and come home to plow the garden on the same day. The dapple-gray mare had soft-looking eyes with white eyelashes. Frida had suggested naming her Velvet, which seemed to fit. The stallion was a copper-colored chestnut with a wide blaze, a white belly spot, and three long stockings—Rob had said they'd been called "high white" back on his home range. After seeing him move, Rob dubbed him Roadrunner.

The mule, however, was too smart for her own good, as most mules are. She knew she didn't have to do anything she didn't want to do, so Kim had been especially liberal with the scratches and treats. Chocolate brown with a light tan muzzle, the mule appeared pleasant enough. One dark spot beneath a nostril resembled a human beauty mark, earning her the name Norma Jean, after a famous actress. If a mule could be elegant, this one was, in sharp contrast to the packhorse they'd named Rat.

Turner had procured three saddles in town, and Frida helped Kim tack up the animals and attach lead ropes for the trip back to Spike City. There, they'd be handed over to the new "recruits," as Stormie was calling the tourists.

Inventories stuffed as full as possible from a night of mining and crafting, Battalion Zero set out on their new mission. Stormie had been reunited with Armor, the black and white paint that enjoyed leading the mounted file. Frida fell in next on Ocelot, with Turner behind them on Duff. Jools guided his palomino, Beckett, next in line, followed by tiny Kim on towering Nightwind. Rob, a restored Saber, and little Rat brought up the rear so the captain could keep an eagle eye on the squadrons before them.

They left the mega taiga behind and rode into a light snowfall upon entering the cold taiga. Frida, who was leading Velvet, noted how softly the white flakes fell on the new horse's nose, resting there gently for a moment before melting away. The survivalist had encountered snow a few times, but she'd never really appreciated its silent persistence before. It was truly beautiful, she thought.

Once underway, Captain Rob ordered the two squadrons to ride boot-to-boot, by twos, and then called for a battalion report. "Turner? Weapons and ammo?"

"Good news and bad news," the sergeant said. "We have more raw materials than finished weaponry. But that's okay. I'ma spend the whole night crafting before tomorrow's train job. Sticks, saplings: check. Cobblestone, flint: check. Short on iron, short on gold, void on feathers. That's bad. Anybody see a chicken, you know what to do."

The cavalry unit had just one long bow, the rustlers' crossbows, two stone swords, six axes, and three remaining pickaxes among them, and one of those was the diamond tool that Crash had anted up the day before. They would need to upgrade and add to their stores, either crafting a ton of arrows or avoiding skeletons at all costs.

"Stormie? Do we have any artillery or trap components at all?" Rob asked.

"Negatory, Captain," she replied. "But I do plan to get some. The creeper that blew back in camp didn't drop any gunpowder, so mining into a dungeon for some should be a top priority. Sand, too, to form TNT—but we ain't gonna find any here on the cold taiga or the ice plains. I asked around in Spike City, and we can hit a mesa plateau to the west or a cold beach to the east for a sand source."

"Meaning, we could also build sand traps," Frida pointed out.

"It'd be nice if we had more spider string for trip wires to augment any traps or explosives," Stormie finished.

"Excellent," Rob said. "I can tell you're on it." He steered Saber around a one-block chunk instead of hopping it, to keep from reinjuring the horse's leg. "Jools? Potions? Supplies?"

Jools had kept a strict watch on the supply chest ever since Turner had helped himself to certain ingredients without permission. "Same as Turner's weapons report," he replied. "We have some brewing ingredients from Colonel M—plenty of Nether wart and some redstone and glowstone dust. Ditto on Stormie's dungeon request; I'll need some gunpowder to make splash potions. Everyone be on the lookout for more sugar, rabbits, or anything a spider might drop."

"Thank you, Quartermaster. How about our food stores?"

"Won't last long." Jools looked worried.

"We'll use some of our advance payments to trade for bread and other vittles in town," Rob said. "Everybody keep an axe handy, and let's hunt down whatever crosses our path."

This suggestion fell flat. No one mentioned the absence of edible wildlife in the snowy biomes, or the presence of predatory wolves.

"We'll be camping west of town in a mountainous region of the cold taiga, en route to our payday rendezvous in the extreme hills," Rob announced. "Vanguard, I'd like a scouting report, then. It will influence our next move with regard to the tourists."

"I believe *recruits* is the more respectful term, sir," Stormie said, only half-joking. "If we make them feel part of the unit, they're more likely to show loyalty if, and when, we need it."

Rob grinned. "Agreed," he said. "And Kim? I'll ask you for a full rundown on the horses once we get the new . . . recruits mounted."

Although nowhere near solid, their position had definitely improved. Hearing this sent a thin but reassuring ray of hope shining down on Frida through the snow-filled sky. She silently renewed her commitment to the group . . . for now.

*

They greeted their motley crew of new recruits at the town well, as arranged.

Judge Tome brightened at the sight of Norma Jean, the mule that Kim was leading. "Now, there's a beautiful female," the gray-haired man said. "I do favor the strong, silent type." Norma Jean let out an open-mouthed bray that caused her to fart and left everyone a little deaf for a moment. "I stand corrected," Judge Tome said, rubbing his ears and waving at the air.

Kim could see the instant attraction, though, and helped him into the mule's saddle, his cloak draping elegantly over the cantle.

De Vries, a tall, stocky player with straight blond hair that hung in his eyes slightly, stood waiting with a bulky inventory bursting with building supplies. He carried so many trapdoors, glass panes, ladders, pistons, and the like that he had no room for weapons or food, Frida noticed.

His sister, Crash, had the same physical substance as De Vries, but less height. Her blonde hair was tamed with a yellow leather cap that sported a tiny redstone lamp on the front. "For mining," De Vries said pointedly when he saw Turner staring jealously at it. Crash's inventory was nearly full of raw blocks of every kind. As they stood around making introductions, Frida and Stormie watched Crash nervously chopping away at the packed ice at her feet and idly adding blocks to her stash. In fact, the ground all around the new recruit had been hacked to a ragged mess.

Seeing the women's expressions, De Vries explained, "Crash never really stops mining. She's a bit of a *knor*."

"What's that?" Stormie asked.

Jools heard them and was familiar with the term. "A type of social misfit," he translated. "In this case, I believe, an ore nerd. It's an honorable obsession. Pleased to make your acquaintance, you two."

Kim took Velvet from Frida and walked the mare and Roadrunner over. De Vries sized them up. "Sort of small, compared to our usual Friesian horses. But they'll do. I like this gray one." He put a foot in Velvet's stirrup and pulled himself into the saddle like a pro. "What say you, sis?"

Crash eyed Roadrunner from under her mining cap. She nodded and got up on the big chestnut, no problem.

All three recruits were experienced riders, so as soon as Turner, Rob, and Jools made a quick trade stop, they all filed up the torch-lined main street and exited at the far end of town.

*

C Squadron, as Rob had dubbed the newbies, was sandwiched between the other two squads as they rode three abreast on horseback. By virtue of his advanced age, Judge Tome was christened a corporal and put in charge of the unit, to which the others agreed. Then Captain Rob repeated their mission and stated the travel rules the cavalry team had drafted.

"Given that we have to act as a unit in case of threat, we'll consider you *ad hoc* members of Battalion Zero," he said.

The judge turned to Rob, who rode on his right. "I see you've studied your Latin, Captain. We'll appreciate the alliance with a learned commander."

Frida was struck by how easy it was for some people to adapt to a group. She glanced over at Crash on the new stallion. The young woman seemed to exist in her own world. Reins in one hand, she never stopped swinging the diamond pickaxe she carried in the other. Her beefy arm had to be its own deadly weapon. *I wouldn't want to meet her in a dark roofed forest*, Frida thought.

Rob was talking to the new travelers about their communal stores. "Now, we can't force you to contribute to the war effort, but anything you do want to share we'll gladly put toward our next campaign on behalf of the United Biomes. In the meantime, we expect you to turn over all foodstuffs and any necessaries for shelter and protection to Quartermaster Jools."

"Will we get a receipt of some kind?" asked De Vries in his musical voice as he guided Velvet up front in between Armor and Beckett.

"The battalion inventory is computerized on a spreadsheet," Jools said, put out by the allusion that he might be less than honest. "I'll expect *you* to sign out anything that you remove."

Okay, so maybe group dynamics aren't built in a day, Frida thought with a smile.

"Corporal Kim will delegate housekeeping and horse-keeping duties, while Turner heads up weapons crafting," Rob continued, not even noticing the ruffled feathers of those at the front of the line. "Everyone must do his or her part."

The conversation paused as the travelers arrived at the north fork of the frozen river, and the riders urged their horses across. Beckett balked a bit, but the first six horses soon stepped onto the iced-over stream, their shod hooves preventing them from sliding. Then Duff and Saber followed Ocelot and Nightwind's lead . . . but Norma Jean would not.

Judge Tome clucked to her and squeezed at her sides with his legs. This urging just made her more uncooperative, her front legs bracing at the snowy edge of the river and her muzzle pooched forward over it, as though to mark the boundary of her good will. Turner and Rob circled Duff and Saber back around, chirruping to the molly mule with no effect but a raised tail and an emission of gas. She stood her ground with a gleam in her eye that said, *Try me.* The others had stopped in the middle of the frozen stream to watch. "This is a case for the bronc whisperer!" Stormie remarked, using the nickname that Kim had earned back when the battalion was first trying to tame wild horses.

Now Kim circled Nightwind, fell even with Norma Jean, and looked her over. "I know what she needs." Kim pulled a carrot from her saddlebag and hung the vegetable from a small length of spider string she'd been saving. Then she handed it to Crash. "If you wouldn't mind tying that onto your pickaxe, I'm sure she'll follow Roadrunner across."

This was no sooner said than done.

"Brilliant!" cheered Jools. "I'd heard about that carrot and stick thing, but I'd never seen it in action."

As they moved off the ice plains toward a mountainous cold taiga, Rob asked Frida to relay their immediate travel plans to the newcomers. "As vanguard," he explained, "Frida is our eyes and ears on the trail. You can trust her with your lives."

Frida blushed a darker shade of green. "Thank you, Captain. Since this is an exploratory mission with work obligations, we'll move in a spiral, starting from Spike City and hitting numerous biomes on this side of the extreme hills. We feel fairly confident that they are free from Lady Craven's mobs."

The newbies mumbled at mention of the notorious griefer queen.

"We'll make camp nightly at a site scouted by me that fills our needs as best it can. Don't have much of a choice tonight, though. Sorry."

"Cold taiga it is," said the judge cheerily.

Frida continued, "You all will hole up in camp or move on to a rendezvous point while one of our squadrons performs whatever job we've secured. Then we'll meet up and move on. Until such time as you folks pick a destination."

"Perhaps *ad infinitum*. . . ." murmured Judge Tome.

"We don't have forever," Rob said. "We intend to travel, take paid work, replenish our inventories, and eventually get back to cavalry business. Anything to add, Vanguard?"

"De Vries and Crash, here, are wanting to homestead. Our next couple of stops will bring us to comfier biomes," Frida assured them. "Stormie, you'll have a chance to mine sand. Turner, you should get a shot at chickens, cows, sheep, and other critters. Everything else, we'll pick up in Spike City—we'll circle around to that village as needed."

The band had begun climbing up snowy blocks as they gained altitude on the taiga. The snowfall had stopped, and all was quiet and still, save for the nine riders, their mounts, and the packhorse that trailed behind Saber.

As their ranks swung around a stand of spruce trees, an animal wail suddenly rang out, answered by several more howls.

"Wolves!" Jools cried, pointing to a pack coming their way. Without thinking, he pulled some dirt blocks from his inventory and threw them at the knot of wild dogs. This set them to snapping their jaws and slouching forward across the snow.

"What'd you do that for?" Kim said. "Now they're hostile!"

The wolves started running, red eyes narrowed, teeth bared, low snarls escaping their throats.

Beckett began to jig, and his fear set Velvet on edge. Stormie put up a hand and reined brave Armor to a stop, but the horses behind her danced and snorted. "What should we do, Captain?" Stormie called.

He cast a glance at Kim, their expert on animal-related matters. "What do you think?"

For once, she was at a loss. The wolves had raced to within a dozen blocks. An attack was coming, and none of the horses wanted to be the victim.

Just then, the two new recruits Crash and De Vries kicked out of their stirrups and jumped down from their tall thoroughbreds. Right before everyone's eyes, their forms began to waver and shift. Their skins darkened, and their clothing slipped to the ground.

Am I seeing this? Frida thought wildly.

The two players had lost their human qualities, and now, right in front of the riders, they each showed four legs, a tail, and triangular ears that stood upright.

CHAPTER 5

HAPE SHIFTERS! FRIDA MENTALLY KICKED HERSELF for not deducing this important fact about the brother-and-sister team before signing them on. She could identify them by the distinctive black diamonds on their foreheads. Now, the question was this: Would they defend the riders or turn on them?

The players' true motives might not determine their next move. Four hostile wolves faced off with the shape shifters, tails rigid. Frida knew that angry wolves could enlist tame ones to do battle. It was all she could do to hold Ocelot steady as the petrified mare tried to rise on her hind legs and free up her front hooves to strike out.

"Captain!" Turner shouted. He had dropped Duff's reins and grasped an axe in either hand. Duff began backing rapidly away from the danger.

Rob, sweating profusely, tried to keep a clear head. He held up a palm, alerting Turner to hold off on an attack. Two axes would not protect them from six wolves.

The next moment, the canines struck. Riders struggled with their horses, watching as the shape shifters hurled themselves at the hostiles, tearing at their throats: one, two, three, four wolves taken out, bloodied, and—then—gone.

Widespread relief could practically be heard in the ensuing silence.

The shape shifters sniffed at the empty ground a few times and then morphed back into their original skins, as though rewinding a film back to its start.

"I don't think this land is quite what we're looking for as far as relocation," De Vries said matter-of-factly. He collected Velvet's reins and remounted. Crash followed his lead on Roadrunner.

Frida eyed Rob and sent him a silent message of apology. Jools hauled the normally slow-moving Beckett back into line opposite Stormie, allowing De Vries to ride in between them, while Frida and Kim wordlessly retook their places on either side of Crash. The rearguard shakily realigned themselves.

"Somethin' you folks weren't telling us?" Turner asked on behalf of the group.

Judge Tome pressed Norma Jean forward. "I think they just did," he said.

De Vries turned in his saddle. "You lot aren't against our kind, are you?"

"Not if you're with us," Kim said. She twisted in Nightwind's saddle to address Rob. "Captain, shape shifters with alternate wolf forms are very rare. They can be quite valuable in certain situations, as you can see." She turned around and spoke to Jools riding in front of her. ". . . like when a player who should know better antagonizes neutral mobs."

"So sorry," Jools muttered. "I don't know what got into me."

"We all make mistakes, Quartermaster," Rob observed.

"Just not potentially deadly ones," Turner accused. "Any one of us could be without a mount right now."

"*Tut, tut*. All's well that ends well," said the judge, trying to ease the tension.

Frida said nothing. Actions spoke louder than words, especially in this situation. Jools had only been defending them, on reflex. The shape shifters had proved their allegiance . . . so far.

The new recruits continued to help out as the day wore on, and the battalion made camp at the boundary where the cold taiga met a mountainous plateau. The carpet beneath their feet now was red sand, not snow, and the foliage had dwindled away to dead bush, the altitude and wind twisting the shrubs into dry sculptures. Although colder, the terrain reminded

Frida of Bryce Mesa without the tall hoodoo rock formations. Before Jools could hand out shovels and pickaxes, De Vries tapped Crash on the shoulder, and she went to work hollowing out a terrace shelter for the horses. Kim helped them place a fence, a gate, and night torches. The string of saddle and pack animals was bedded down in record time.

Frida and Stormie were trying to choose a shelter site when De Vries again patted his sister and pointed at the sheer cliff wall. In seconds, she had carved out an entrance and begun tunneling deeper into the rock. The survivalist and the adventurer shrugged at each other and went to get dinner and fire materials from the quartermaster.

With dusk coming on, Battalion Zero's six original members gathered around the campfire, as they had so many times since they had formed an alliance. *But times clearly have changed,* Frida thought as she watched Judge Tome pull up a rock and plop down on it. He mumbled a few words of thanks to the world generator for providing bread and pork chops before digging in to his plate.

Turner elbowed Frida. "Was *me* traded for that food in town," he pointed out.

"Poor Meat," she teased him. "Using other people's emeralds to buy yourself dinner. And not even a thank you. . . ."

He elbowed her harder, and she fell over, just as De Vries and Crash approached the campfire. Crash reached her pickaxe arm forward and pulled Frida up with her pinky finger. Frida grinned. *Holy end stone! I knew she was strong.*

Jools had fetched water from a nearby stream and offered everyone a drink. "I propose a toast," he said, and they all came to attention. "To our new C Squadron. They've proven useful already."

"To C Squadron!" the veterans chorused.

"*Useful* is Jools's highest compliment," Stormie told the newbies. "And I'm much obliged for any shelter building . . . or wolf killing," she added.

Turner glanced at the judge. "What good's he done?"

"It's not what he's done." Jools set his water bucket down. "It's what he's about to do."

Judge Tome's expression showed that even he didn't know what he was about to do that would deserve a toast from Jools.

"Let me ask you this, mate," the quartermaster addressed him. "Have you ever bent the law in order to uphold it?"

He acknowledged that he had.

"Well, Your Lordship, that is what this battalion is about to do."

Frida saw where Jools was leading. "Stealing from the rich, giving to the poor," she said. "Not exactly a heinous griefer crime. But not strictly legal, either."

"Some leverage might be obtained from the hand of law," Jools continued. "We do still have your UBO ring. If we need to throw some legal weight around, would you play that role?"

All eyes went to the federation judge.

The man spread his hands. "I'd like to assist, but as you know, Overworld law has been severely undermined by Lady Craven's rebels. It's my reason for . . . retiring."

Now Rob stepped in. "We respect your privacy, sir. But your air of authority might tip the scales in our favor, at some point."

Stormie spoke up. "Seeing as how our fortunes are all linked right now, playing judge could save your skin, too."

This sank in, and Judge Tome relented. "Well, for the good of the company . . ."

*

Night fell, and the players blocked themselves inside the cliff dwelling that Crash and De Vries had built. When the sun rose, A Squadron left the others there to craft weapons while they went to meet up with Bluedog a short ride away.

Frida walked Ocelot along behind Stormie and Armor. Heading toward the back side of the extreme hills—not far from the site of their recent crushing defeat—they were glad to have Turner along with most of their arsenal. Frida suspected that Jools, Rob, and Kim were equally happy to have remained in camp.

They picked their way up the mountain terrace and reined over to the coordinates that Rafe had provided. Someone was already there.

Frida recognized the black and purple frame of a Nether portal but not the face of the man guarding it. His skin was blue-and-white striped, and his eyes were set too closely together, causing them to appear crossed. It was hard to know what he was looking at.

Turner legged Duff over to the man and relayed the password that Rafe had provided: *Alpha 6*.

"Vanilla 9," came the reply that identified the man as Bluedog. "We have a deal." He gave Turner a handful of diamonds as a down payment.

"When do we see the rest?" Turner demanded.

Bluedog put a paw on the side of the Nether portal. "When the supply train loot is poured through this. If you don't bring it back safely, you don't get paid."

Turner pulled out a piece of paper with a mark on it. "And if we don't get paid, we'll get a warrant for your arrest so fast it'll make your compass spin."

Bluedog scrutinized the stamp made by Judge Tome's ring. He didn't appear too upset. "Making legal threats is not the best insurance, friend." He stepped back and raised a wool sheet to reveal a cage filled with a thick mob of chittering arthropods. They flitted angrily into the bars, eager to escape and attack.

Frida shuddered at the sight of a broken monster egg lying amid the tiny mobsters in the cage. *I hate silverfish,* she thought. *No wonder Xanto never leaves the jungle.* The battalion hadn't been plagued by any of the bug-like monsters during their attack on the zombies' stronghold, but she knew the extreme hills were rife with the creatures. Perhaps this Bluedog had rounded them all up. She shuddered again. Once loosed, they might never stop spawning.

Turner paid them no mind. "Just tell us where to meet the train."

Bluedog gave the coordinates. "Ride alongside those rails, and you can't miss it. Fellow name of Mad Jack will be driving. And don't get any ideas. All the loot is locked in a chest via enchantment. Driver carries no cash."

Stormie recorded their current position and the rendezvous point on her map, and they set off into the steep terrain that was broken only by a few brown trees. The band was very near the place where Stormie had lost her life in the fateful battle.

Frida cut her a look. "Stay frosty. Don't let the location get to you."

"Thanks, Frida."

Armor, Ocelot, and Duff climbed so steadily that, before long, they moved into the clouds that shrouded the landscape. "This puts the *extreme* in hills," Turner commented. "How'd they ever lay this track?"

Thick cloud cover reduced the sunlight to dangerous levels. Sure enough, before the squadron had even reached their meeting place, the familiar groan of shade-loving zombies floated their way. "Uuuuhh-*uh-uh!* Ooohhh-*oh-oh!*"

"Those echoes make it sound like twice as many zombies as there really are," Frida complained.

"Better use double the weapons, then," Turner advised, tossing her an extra sword. "These things are old and liable to break."

Then they heard a hacking sound and a man's shout. "I'll tear off yer limbs, put 'em back, and rip 'em off again!" he threatened.

They topped a rise and emerged from the wrap of clouds to see a grizzled, bearded fellow perched on a mine cart chest using two swords lashed end to end to push zombies away from the track. Sunshine broke through the wispy haze, and the green, rotting monsters burned up and disappeared.

Frida jumped down from Ocelot and gathered the vegetables and flesh that they dropped, offering them to the minecart driver.

"Keep 'em." He waved her off. "I only eat fresh meat."

"Right on," said Stormie. "An anti-vegetarian. You must be Mad Jack."

"'Tis I," said the old codger. "Forgive me if I do not extend a hand, but I dasn't get out of this cart. Whole thing's computerized. If she stops, I won't know how to get moving again." The cart inched along on the first piece of flat ground the squadron had hit thus far. Here, the unfiltered sun had reduced the scattered spruce trees to dead sticks.

The three troopers spread out behind the cart, one on either side and Ocelot's rider picking her way between the cart tracks. Then the rails followed the terrain, which fell away steeply where they had just made their ascent.

Down is even harder than up, Frida realized. She had a clear view of the back of Mad Jack's neck, a sweaty region populated by wiry gray hair. It was going to be a long ride back.

"Whereabouts you from, pardners?" the cart driver asked.

"Here and there," Stormie said. "We're short of cash on our way south."

Turner had instructed the two women to ask no questions and tell only lies. "Mercenaries' code," he'd said.

"Headin' south . . . sounds like my ownself as a young 'un. These days, though, a reg'lar paycheck is more appealing than boundary surveyin'."

"I get where you're coming from," Turner replied conversationally. "But I have a problem showing up at the office, if you know what I mean."

"That I do. That I do."

Frida sorted through this information for answers to the questions she couldn't ask. A regular paycheck meant that he came through this way like clockwork. That meant that whatever he was transporting— and Rafe had let on that it was gemstones and other valuables—was generated on a regular basis. Could it be the loot that Legs and his crew shook down the villagers for in Lady Craven's name? If so, was Legs behind this shipment to the Nether? Or had someone else sidetracked the cartful of goodies? And which gang was Bluedog working for?

"Looks like a peaceful trip," Stormie remarked.

"Gen'rally. Least ways, until all hell breaks loose."

Instinctively, Frida checked over her shoulder. But nothing was following them that she could detect. Her thoughts floated back to that tactical error made during her clan's freedom test. "Sergeant!" she called. "Best keep an eye for pressure plates."

"Mm-hmm," Stormie said. "Could trigger an explosion or an avalanche."

"Wish to avoid suchlike. That's what Bluedog pays you fer," murmured Mad Jack.

"Ain't been paid yet," Turner pointed out.

"All in good time."

They rode on in silence awhile, the computer now applying a brake instead of a boost on the steep incline. Ocelot spooked when some loose gravel beneath her feet gave way, and Frida got a scare as she tipped forward precipitously. But the mare quickly regained her footing and proceeded more carefully downward.

At last they came toward the colorful Nether portal frame, which was easy to spot from the bare hillside. Frida realized she'd been holding her breath, and she relaxed as the air whooshed out.

There was Bluedog waiting for them. The silverfish lying in the cage next to him roused when they saw the players approaching and buzzed angrily against the bars once more. Frida couldn't wait to leave them behind.

The horses and riders stopped and paused while Mad Jack transferred the precious chest to their employer. Bluedog produced a key and opened it. He pawed through the contents and tossed Turner an assortment of gems, which he caught one at a time and stashed in his saddlebag.

"Nice riding with you!" Stormie tipped her head at the minecart driver.

"Same here," he said and boosted the cart back up the hill on its powered rails.

Meanwhile, Bluedog emptied the chest into the Nether portal, where its contents disappeared in a sprinkling of purple particles.

"We can do business again," he said. "Be here in seven days."

"I'll talk to my boss," Turner said.

He, Frida, and Stormie turned back toward camp, not saying much until they were out of Bluedog's earshot.

"That was easy," Stormie said, as though there were something wrong with *easy.*

Turner shot her a look. "That's the way I like it."

Frida made no comment. In her experience, nothing easy paid well. And nothing that paid well was ever as simple as it looked.

CHAPTER 6

ASQUADRON FOUND THE REMAINDER OF Battalion Zero enjoying domestic bliss back at camp on the plateau. To Frida's amazement, they rode up to see Kim exercising two of the new horses in a professional-looking arena decorated with potted shrubbery. A wooden riser provided seating for spectators, and a variety of jump obstacles in the ring promised something to see.

Frida, Stormie, and Turner tied their mounts to the rail and joined the others in the viewing stands. Kim had treated them to her trick riding before, but this performance was even more impressive. Velvet led Roadrunner around the pen, trotting a circle around Kim, who stood in the middle. The horse master's glossy black hair was covered by a pink cap that matched her skin, and one golden earring dangled beneath it. She held a long stick—one without a carrot at the end as bait. When she raised the stick at an angle, the horses moved into a faster canter and then leaped over the three jump rails, each one set higher than the last.

Then Kim walked toward the animals, and they stepped away from her, changing direction. Folks in the stands clapped. As the horses completed a circuit, Kim blocked their path and then backed off, causing them to head to the center of the circle. "And, ho!" she called. Velvet halted and effectively stopped Roadrunner in his tracks.

Kim moved in front of them and raised her arms and the stick as though asking an orchestra for a fanfare. The horses reared in tandem and hovered a moment, until Kim dropped her arms. They settled back to earth, standing with eyes and ears on their leader. She reached out with her stick and tapped the ground. Velvet stretched out a foreleg and dipped her head and neck down in a bow. Roadrunner followed suit.

The stands erupted in applause, and Kim curtsied.

Frida felt a jab in her side. It was Crash, who sat next to her on the bottom plank. She tilted her head at Kim, who was climbing over the arena railing.

Frida understood. "Kim says she learned her magic with horses just by watching them."

Crash appeared to admire this. *She knows the value of observation,* Frida thought. *And hard work.* Frida chuckled, noticing the semicircular moat Crash had dug in the dirt with her pickaxe as she watched the show.

"You're a good rider, by the way," Frida complimented the miner. "I think Roadrunner was the right choice for you. He's fast and strong."

Crash smiled for the first time that Frida had seen. Then she got up and went to pet her horse, which stood waiting for more attention at the arena fence.

"What's all this?" Frida asked Kim when she approached.

"De Vries said he had a vision when he saw me working Nightwind on his lead line. He's an awesome builder. How'd the job go?"

"Over and out. A little bit richer." Frida grinned. "What's our next move?"

"The horses need grass. And we've got to pay the farmer for those mounts we appropriated. And locate some chickens! Shorter answer: we're heading south. There's a mountain savanna between our original camp and the plains. We're going to explore it while the horses fatten up."

"And *we* fatten up," Frida added. "Should be able to find all the food groups there."

"Food—what?" Jools said, walking past with his water bucket. "I'm literally craving a shepherd's pie."

"*Baa-a-a!*" Kim mimicked a sheep, and Jools pantomimed drawing his sword and slaughtering her.

"She died for a good cause," he said rubbing his belly and walking off.

Stormie caught Frida's attention. "Girl, you have got to see this!" She walked up and steered the vanguard toward the rock shelter, which Crash had started the night before.

The entrance had been fortified with cobblestone and an iron gate designed to echo the arched doorway.

"Wipe your feet!" Stormie said, pointing out the carpet square that served as a welcome mat.

Inside, the vestibule reminded Frida of Colonel M's imposing foyer—without the back wall grate that confined wither skeletons. In its place was a massive waterfall fountain that drained into a pool below. The only thing missing was some goldfish. Frida followed Stormie through a hallway that led deeper into the rock and split off into side rooms.

"Count 'em! Ten!" Stormie said. "We each get our own room, plus a kitchen room for crafting."

"De Vries again?"

"He's thought of everything," Stormie marveled.

They peeked into the many rooms that were furnished with chairs and desks, and the common area that held a furnace and crafting table.

"Everything's here but beds," Frida noted.

"That's because I don't sleep," came De Vries's voice from behind them. "I forget that other players do."

"Well, it's a nice way to end the day. . . ." Stormie said.

Frida never slept in a bed. She had no wish to change her original spawn point and wouldn't discuss that secret jungle location with anyone. "I love what you've done with the entryway," Frida mentioned to De Vries as they strolled back out.

Two circles had been hollowed out of the rock high above the doorway, and blue glass panes set into them. The sunlight passing through made two large, blue dots on the opposite wall that shifted as clouds floated past.

"Thanks," said De Vries. "I figure, if you're going to spend the night, *spend the night.*" He sat down on a couch he had crafted and put his feet up on a carpet-topped ottoman.

"Leave for ten minutes and see what happens," Frida joked to Stormie on their way outside.

"Vanguard! Artilleryman! I've been looking for you," Captain Rob said.

"We can see you've been super busy while we were off bodyguarding," Stormie teased, causing the cowboy's cheeks to color.

"Let's sit down and debrief." He headed back toward the stadium seats, calling the quartermaster, who also acted as war strategist, to confer. Jools joined them.

"Turner says you were successful," Rob said, addressing the two women. "Can you confirm that he turned over the payment to Jools in total?"

They compared notes. There was the handful of diamonds . . . and Frida recalled Bluedog throwing seven chunks to the sergeant major afterward.

"Was one of them a chunk of dirt?" Jools scratched his head as he studied the spreadsheet opened on his computer.

"No." Frida scowled. Her friend tended to line his pockets whenever he got a chance.

Rob sighed. "And Bluedog? He fulfilled his end of the bargain?"

"It was half in advance, and half when the job was done, sir," Stormie verified.

"Any sense of his reliability?" Rob asked Frida.

She thought it over. "Based on what we heard from the minecart driver, the loot comes through the same channels regularly. So the job seems like a sure thing. This Bluedog, though . . . I'm not sure which side he's playing. What I do know is, he's dangerous."

"Second that," Stormie said.

"Well, that's why the job pays," Rob reminded everyone. "Okay, we'll accept the offer for the next gig. Turner says it's going to be every seven days." Rob paused. "Unfortunately, that won't keep us in pork chops. We've got a battalion to feed. Working once a week won't cut it and still let us build up our war chest."

Again, Frida lamented the group dynamic that consumed so many resources. If it were just herself in the jungle . . .

"Vanguard, talk to your brother and see what else he can rustle up. You'll have to pay him his cut from yesterday, too. Why don't you two deal with that in Spike City while we ride south? We'll meet at our old stone shelter and move on together from there."

Frida saluted. "Yes, sir."

Jools tapped his computer screen. "About this dirt clod, Captain . . ."

Rob sighed again and called, "Turner!" He surveyed the camp but did not locate the sergeant at arms. "Has anyone seen Turner?"

Nobody had.

*

They checked among the horses. Duff had been fed and watered, and his rider was not nearby. Stormie used the hunt as an excuse to tour their rock dwelling again, but Turner was not in any of its ten well-designed rooms. They asked Crash, who was idly harvesting and storing red sand, if she had seen the sergeant major; she had not.

Fearing that Bluedog or one of Precious's gang had something to do with the disappearance, Rob finally called the rest of the battalion together to walk the area perimeter. In a short time, they heard splashing. They marched around a corner to find the AWOL sergeant seated on a riverbank, fishing.

"I got one!" Turner cried as he spied the search party. He unhooked a piece of rotten flesh and added it to the pile of junk he had scored with his fishing pole.

Frida tightened her fists. She and Stormie had completed their part of the mission without a bonus of any sort. But an extra diamond or lapis block wasn't enough for the mercenary.

She got a running start, locked her arms in front of her, and shoved Turner into the blue water. Down he went, out of sight. Then his head popped up, and he flailed his arms, yelling, "I c-can't swim!"

Rob threw Frida a bewildered glance. After letting Turner flounder a bit, the survivalist hopped into the water and swam for the drowning man. He coughed and gagged as she held his head above water in the crook of one arm, his dark buzz cut wet and shining. She scissor-kicked her way back to shore, heaving her human load up onto the red sand and then pulling herself out of the water.

Turner lay gasping next to his catch, his tattooed arms gritty with sand. "What's the big deal!" he puffed.

"Stealing from company stores again, eh, Meat?" Jools said, crossing his arms and staring at the disgraced officer.

"It weren't stealing," Turner argued, breathing heavily. He got to his feet and faced the quartermaster. "And you don't get to call me Meat."

Jools was livid. "Meat. Ham. Chicken. Pork Chop. I'll call you whatever I please."

". . . and subtract a lapis lazuli out of his pay when it comes due," Rob added. He shook his head. "I'm afraid you've earned a court-martial, Sergeant Major."

Surprise, shame, and then justification flowed through Turner's eyes. "I was just taking my advance. Mebbe shouldn't have. . . . Don't you military types have to call a trial to bust a man?"

Judge Tome walked up. "You are correct, sir. I'll be happy to preside," he said with a smile, and Rob shook his hand.

The battalion milled around the riverbank, each of the officers struck once more by Turner's greed. De Vries, his brow wrinkled with worry, put up a hand. "I'd like to know how we can trust this man, Captain."

Rob pressed his lips together. "So would I." He faced Turner. "You'll spend some time as a private. Frida will command your squadron. I'm upgrading her to corporal."

Frida could scarcely appreciate this honor when faced with disappointment in her old friend and adversary.

Rob waved a hand at the loot Turner had reeled in. "Somebody put this stuff away."

Crash laid a hand on her brother's arm and pointed at the rotten flesh that had been dredged up from the water.

"Anybody going to eat that?" De Vries interpreted in his sing-song voice.

Everyone stared dumbly.

"I'll pass," said Turner.

Rob blew up. "It's not for you to say!" He looked at De Vries. "Don't think so. That stuff'll make you sick."

Crash raised her eyebrows at her brother.

"But it won't make a wolf sick," he said, grinning. Then he and Crash morphed into their alternate skins and devoured the piece of meat.

*

Frida and Stormie returned to Spike City to conduct company business while the rest of Battalion Zero recycled De Vries's building materials and rode south. Ocelot and Armor walked amiably side by side into another snow flurry, carrying the survivalist and the adventurer toward the ice plains city. Rafe needed to be compensated and queried about more work.

Trades would be made for essentials. Jools had asked for some glass bottles and fermented spider eye for his brewing kit, and Kim wanted a new leather halter for Rat, since leading him had worn out his old one. De Vries and Crash asked for some redstone, and Rob and Judge Tome requested some fresh produce from the town's covered garden. Only Turner's bid for arrow crafting materials from the fletcher was denied. They would soon be able to gather feathers from chickens in the milder climes themselves, and Crash's nonstop mining had yielded a nice supply of flint. Rob reminded the troopers that in order to build their wealth, they had to limit their spending.

"He's so danged practical," Stormie said to Frida, mixing her complaint with admiration.

Ocelot carefully stepped over a wayward ice chunk. "*Practical* is what kept Newbie alive for his first few days in the Overworld," Frida replied. "But sometimes it limits what he can do." *Like have a girlfriend.*

They reached the north gate of town and waved at the snow golem, who let them pass. Then they split up—Stormie going to make trades and Frida off to speak to her brother . . . alone.

It seemed awfully improbable to have met him after all these years, out here on the world fringe, well connected with small-time riffraff yet in a position of relative trading authority. As he had said, his cleric's robe lent him leeway, allowing him to make less-than-scrupulous deals. *Funny that our battalion would need that, and here he is.* Frida had often wondered over the years what had become of her brothers and male cousins. She may well have met them before and not recognized them as clan members, but this time. . . She wanted to get to the bottom of Rafe's tattoo history.

She knocked on the ice chapel door, and her brother opened it. His hair was pulled back in a greasy ponytail that hung like a limp serpent against his worn purple robe. They feinted a few punches in greeting.

"So, sister of mine," Rafe said, ushering her into the main hall. "You've brought my commission?" She handed him two emeralds. "One for the first haul, one in advance for the second. Bluedog gave us a nod, so our captain has agreed to hire on regular for as long as it works out. We could use a few side jobs, though."

"Your gang is headed south?" Rafe said. "The syndicate is looking for a pickup team from farmers in the plains, savanna, and nearby forests."

Frida frowned. "Syndicate . . . are they allied with the griefer army?"

Rafe shook his head. "They're offering protection to farmers and villagers from the griefers. While skimming some of their wares off the top, of course."

Collecting strong-arm protection money was hardly an honest way to make a living. Frida was sad to think the battalion had come to such dire straits, but it would all be conducted in the name of Overworld peace, she reminded herself.

"Who's our contact?"

"The same."

"Bluedog, again?" She shivered, remembering the extortionist's captive silverfish.

Rafe regarded her with amusement. "Frida. This is Spike City. The area is hardly awash in gainful employment." He rose and went to a side table for a bottle of blue liquid. "Flower water?" he said, offering her some refreshment.

She tried not to appear suspicious. Poison or a potion of weakness could easily be dyed an identical shade. She accepted the drink, wetting her lips. "Get us the pickup coordinates and drop point," Frida said. "We'll appreciate the steady work."

He returned the bottle to the table, and she could see the tattoo of the arrow-impaled apple on the back of his neck once more, peeking out from his ponytail. "Brotherman," she said casually, "how'd you get your family mark? I was under the impression that only girls got them, and only after passing the freedom test."

He turned toward her with an illicit smile and wagged the end of his ponytail. "Comes in handy as a disguise." He fingered the folds of his robe. "I've already got the dress."

His meaning dawned on her. "Are you saying you crashed Apple Corps?" That was the name of the family rally so secret that its location was only divulged on the day of the event.

Rafe looked at her evenly.

"*And* you passed a freedom test? As a girl?"

This was impossible! How could a child who was sent away from the clan have acquired the necessary level of survival skills?

"But how?" she demanded.

"It's called acting," he said condescendingly.

She had no choice but to buy his explanation. The preposterous story increased her desire to return to her jungle family to see for herself that they were okay.

Rafe went to his computer to contact Bluedog and nail down the job for Frida's battalion. He returned and handed her a card imprinted with the likeness of a blue hunting dog. *Much more handsome than the actual guy,* she thought. They were to display the card as proof of their representation in demanding the required protection payments. Once gathered, the goods should be brought to their next rendezvous at the extreme foothills. Frida had Rafe forward the pickup locations to Jools electronically and then promised to see him in a week.

As she waited at the town well for Stormie, Frida mulled over the meeting. It had only provoked more questions. How had Rafe known her unit was riding south? She hadn't mentioned it. What was Rafe's relationship with Bluedog, and how far did the extortionist's reach extend? And—most perplexing—how did Rafe really get that tattoo?

CHAPTER 7

FRIDA AND STORMIE CROSSED THE FROZEN RIVER and tracked across the cold taiga, riding south.

"I hope we don't run into any more wolves," Frida said. "You're lucky Armor is so steadfast. Ocelot about blew a gasket last time."

"I'm pretty sure the two of us could outrun any wolves. But remember, if we don't bother them, we should be safe."

Poor Jools. He'd never forget that slip-up. *Neither will Turner,* Frida thought, wondering how the deposed sergeant was taking his probation.

They found out upon meeting the battalion at their old mega taiga shelter. De Vries had crafted three wooden stands and a bench to accommodate the court-martial proceedings. As soon as witnesses Frida and Stormie arrived, they began.

Kim seated a sullen Turner on one of the stands, and Judge Tome, in his cloak, took his place up front. Then Kim read the charges: "Sergeant Major Turner is accused of one count failure to release valuables to quartermaster, one count theft, and one count absent without leave. How plead you?"

"Innocent," Turner grunted, folding his decorated arms.

Jools strode forward. He asked Frida to take the stand and describe the exchange of gems between Bluedog and Turner. She repeated what she had told the captain the day before, and Jools dismissed her. He put Stormie through the same routine.

Then Jools smoothed the lapels of his tweed jacket and addressed Turner. "How is it that a block of dirt came to be placed in communal inventory among the payment accounted for? Did you put it there?"

"Dunno."

"Answer *yes* or *no*," Judge Tome directed.

"Not that I know of. Er, no. That is, I coulda picked up some dirt along with what I handed over."

"And did you not *count* the gems you released?" Jools pressed, knowing that Turner continually counted his riches.

"Mebbe."

"*Yes* or *no*," the judge insisted.

"Yes," Turner mumbled. "Coulda miscounted."

"Permission to approach the bench."

The judge nodded, and Jools stepped up with a block of lapis. "Exhibit A," he said. "This was found in Sergeant Major Turner's helmet. It is the exact amount missing from the train job fee."

The questioning repeated the pattern, with Jools suggesting obvious guilt and Turner denying it or, at least, refusing to accept responsibility for it.

Finally, Judge Tome gathered up some paperwork and placed it in his briefcase, saying, "I have no alternative but to issue a court-martial. As suggested by your commanding officer, you will be relieved of your station and act as a private until such time as you have redeemed yourself."

"Do I get to stay in camp and crochet doilies, then?" Turner groused.

Rob could contain himself no longer. He jumped to his feet and said, "No, you do not! Theft or no theft, Turner, you're still our strongest weapons man. This battalion needs your skill in crafting and in fighting, and you know darn well that you can't do either of those things halfway. Now: Will we have your cooperation?"

The question hung in the air. Frida knew that, like herself, Turner had survived prior to the griefer war by *not* cooperating with others—by going it alone and living by his wits. She felt a little bit sorry for him, knowing how hard it was to devote his allegiance, let alone his loot, to the group. But she had done it. He could step up to the plate and do it, too. She caught his eye and let him know as much, silently.

"Yessir," Turner mumbled. As uncharacteristic as cavalry life was for him, he knew that the existence of the United Biomes might well depend on his participation.

Judge Tome whacked the table before him with a wooden axe. "Court-martial adjourned," he said.

As they dispersed, Stormie tried to cheer Turner up. "It's not so bad, Meat. Frida will handle the squadron. Now you can just cruise and let a woman tell you what to do."

He grimaced. "We ain't married, ya know." Then he gave Stormie a playful pop on the shoulder. "And that's Private Meat, to you."

Whatever the mercenary's shortcomings were, he knew when he was beat.

*

It was late afternoon by the time the battalion had crossed the mega taiga boundary and selected a suitable spot to bivouac for a few days. The mountain savanna unfolded dramatically, with thick grass growing shoulder-high and the tree line strung out above them. Rocky towers seemed to erupt from the ground, forming cliffsides that stretched all the way to the low-flying clouds. They could use the temporary camp for several things—as a base between money pickups, a place to drill with the new recruits, and a source of free grazing for the horses.

Rob pointed De Vries and Crash toward a sheer cliff, the interior of which might yield any number of ores and stones, and double as another cave dwelling. "Go nuts," he said.

Everyone found something useful to do. A parade of passive mobs wandered through camp as the building progressed and the sun dipped in the sky. Frida, Stormie, and Turner played target practice with most of them, adding bits of pig, sheep, rabbit, and chicken to their collective inventory. Jools, clearly wanting to avoid Turner, helped Kim craft a corral for the mule and horses out in the tall grass. Rob and Judge Tome built pits for a few of the chickens and sheep that they would keep for their eggs and wool.

The three hunters had put away their swords for the day when a large grayish-white bunny with red eyes hopped across the clearing. It had been a long day for A Squadron, given the draining business in town and at the court-martial, and its members were slightly less sharp than usual. The fluffy mobster sized them up, then targeted the weakest as its prey.

Turner's health bar had tapered after his near drowning and the mental stress of the trial. The killer bunny approached quickly, and before Turner could identify the threat, lunged to attack.

"*Aaugh!*" Turner collapsed in the grass.

Every available trooper heard the cry, but the closest was De Vries, who had walked off and left Crash drilling into the cliffside. Instantly, the builder became wolf, and the wolf engaged the rabid rabbit in a wild melee. Frida had retrieved her sword but knew that close combat with this cottontail could turn fatal fast. In any case, she could not tell where wolf ended and bunny began in the snarling, leaping, tumbling mass of fur.

It took several direct hits from De Vries's wolf form to slay the mobster. By this time, everyone had gathered at a safe distance. They now crept forward, Kim to see to Turner, Crash to help her brother regain his skin, and Jools to collect the rabbit's foot that the expiring animal dropped.

"Potion of leaping, anyone?" The quartermaster was excited to have found the rare brewing item.

"Something healing would be better," said Kim, motioning for help in moving the unresponsive Turner.

Stormie knelt down to check his pulse. She indicated that it was steady but barely there. "The Killer Bunny of Caerbannog," she whispered. "I've been all

over the world and have never seen it strike before."
She approached De Vries, who was rebuttoning his
safari jacket. "Are you all right?"

He seemed to take the fight in stride. "Toppie," he
replied in his musical manner, apparently unhurt. "I
wouldn't mind rabbit stew for dinner, though. I didn't
get a bite before it dissolved."

*

De Vries was the toast of the table that night. Turner
had been patched up and propped up long enough to
taste some of the stew that Kim had prepared.

"Am I eating . . . whatever did this?" Turner asked,
tenderly touching his wounded side.

They let him think so and watched his esteem for
De Vries visibly build.

"So, how's that shape-shifting work?" Turner
asked, curious.

"Yes, have you always had that ability?" Jools
wanted to know.

Crash nodded proudly and showed with her hand
that they'd been able to shape-shift since they were
pup high.

De Vries chuckled. "We used to play tricks on
our teachers in school. They had no clue how wolves
ended up at our desks."

Crash mimed a whistle blower.

"Yes, they even called the police once to look for the missing children . . . us."

"Not everyone tolerates wolves," Judge Tome observed. "Have you had any close calls?"

Crash rolled her eyes.

"Too many to count," said her brother.

Frida knew this meant they were experienced fighters, and she was impressed.

Rob was thinking that their reflexes would make them useful in emergencies. "Have you ever thought of joining the cavalry? As humans," he added.

Crash consulted De Vries hopefully.

"We might."

"Well, we have some training to do," the captain said. Then he turned to Judge Tome. "Even though you're an honorary corporal, it's not right to expect you to join us when you've just retired. But now that we have some weapons and the makings of some ammunition, we should practice skirmishing techniques. You never know what we'll come up against on the trail. Have you ever carried a weapon, Judge?"

The law officer's eyes twinkled. "From time to time. I understand the need, Captain. If you'll provide me a sidearm, I'll learn to use it."

So, they reserved the next two days for mounted and infantry drill. De Vries had built a watchtower with a balcony in the rock. When dusk fell, they dumped gravel and sand from above on the creepers and zombies that clustered at their door, improving their aim and suffocating the monsters for their drops. In between the more dangerous mob spawns, they dashed down to attack spiders for their string. When skeletons appeared, though, they sought safety indoors. De Vries and Crash offered to morph and chase them away, but Rob reckoned that their wolf forms had done enough for the battalion lately.

He was interested in gauging their skill with weapons when they assembled the next day at the area that had been cleared by the creepers' sand-dampened explosions. Squadrons A and B demonstrated cavalry maneuvers on horseback first, with the goal of teaching the others transport and battle formations.

Once mounted, even Norma Jean, the mule, was amenable to walking, trotting, and cantering by file and by twos. With a little practice, they were all striding forward abreast in a phalanx—the mounted version of linking arms and trampling everything in their path.

When they paused for a breather, Crash socked Frida in the arm and gave her an enthusiastic grin.

"It *is* fun, isn't it?" *At least, it is in broad daylight, without any hostile mobs to worry about*, Frida thought.

Rob must have read her mind. "Enjoy it while you can, troops! We'll be practicing this by moonlight pretty soon. Then we'll see how effective we are against the undead and pesky exploding creepers."

It was time to throw weapons into the mix. "Turner! Arm C Squadron with our old swords and bows while Kim and I set up targets."

Rob borrowed Kim's golden earring for use as a bull's-eye. He jabbed a sapling into the dirt at one end of the clearing and hung the gold hoop from it. The troopers were to gallop at the target from a ways off and run their sabers through the dangling band. Wool from their sheep had been wrapped around bales of dry grass and hung from several more saplings to mimic bodies to stab at. For bow practice, they would let loose a few captive rabbits to use as moving targets.

Crash went first. Frida was not surprised that her sword arm was both strong and true. It pierced the fake bodies and ran through the earring with single slashes. However, the miner's aim had previously been focused on stationary blocks. She did not do as well with bow and arrow, managing to clip only one bunny on the ear, shooting from Roadrunner's back.

"Practice that exercise from the ground for a while, Private Crash," Rob advised.

Then De Vries tried his luck. He couldn't skewer the earring on any pass, even when he slowed Velvet to a walk. It was almost embarrassing to watch him attack the woolen bodies, which he only managed to strike with his sword after he got off his horse and ran right up to them. His mind was better suited to geometry than ramming things with sharpened sticks. He excelled at estimating an arrow's trajectory against gravity and wind forces. He nearly decimated their domestic rabbit population before Kim called him off.

"Good work, Private De Vries," Frida encouraged him, making a mental note of his strengths and weaknesses. Now that she was a corporal, she might wind up giving him orders in a melee. If they got caught in hand-to-hand combat, he'd be a goner.

The judge was next up. He pulled his sword and clucked to Norma Jean. Away they sailed at the dangling gold ring. To everyone's dismay, though, he could not skewer it. He gritted his teeth and came at the earring time and again, slicing the air nowhere near it.

"Never mind!" Jools called. "Try the body targets!"

Norma Jean gamely galloped right at the stand-ins for zombie or griefer bodies that might need killing, but Judge Tome could do little more than scrape at them, when he hit them at all.

"Arm rigid!" Rob coached. "Look at Crash!"

She demonstrated a lunge with her pickaxe arm, but the judge's limb had all the rigor of a wet noodle.

"Never mind, Judge," Stormie said, handing him his bow and a few arrows. "You'll do better with these."

He did not. In fact, Stormie and Turner had to duck when his aim went completely awry and their last two bunnies hopped away to nibble on grass.

"Where'd ya learn to fight like that, Judge?" Turner needled him as he collected the weapons.

Judge Tome had no comeback. He appeared contrite but determined to give it another try later.

"You know," Jools said, escorting him away from the drill field, "a lack of proficiency with weapons is not the worst thing on earth. I've found that one stays alive much longer if one never fights in the first place."

Rob overheard him and glared.

"But . . . I've changed my tune somewhat recently," Jools amended.

CHAPTER 8

WEAPONS, AMMO, AND ARMOR CRAFTING commenced the following day with enthusiasm, now that Turner had fully recovered from his rabbit attack. The whole battalion gathered outside the cliff dwelling and spread out to focus on their tasks. The arms expert instructed Judge Tome and Kim in bow construction, making sure they reinforced the compact bow bellies with plenty of spider string. Frida and Rob were allowed to craft arrows from the now-abundant feathers and other materials, subject to Turner's approval. Projectiles that did not meet his standards were broken over his knee and the ingredients recycled for another try at perfection.

De Vries was put to work smelting the iron, gold, and diamond ore that Crash continued to unearth even as she stood otherwise idly by.

"Thank goodness we have a use for this stuff," the builder said, busily manning the furnace. "Sometimes we have to just give it away, my *knor* of a sister stacks so much of it."

Crash smiled sheepishly from beneath her yellow cap. Her route through camp on any given day could be traced by the jagged trenches that she notched with her restless pickaxe.

The ore became sword and axe blades and chest plates on De Vries's crafting table, but he suggested approaching the village armorer in Spike City for additional pieces. "I'm no good at helmets or boots," he admitted. "Ask me to build a cathedral, though, and it's yours."

Rob acknowledged his architectural prowess but posed the need for more practical structures. "We're going to want dozens of chests and extra carts to carry Bluedog's loot to the hills."

Meanwhile, Jools toyed with his brewing ingredients. He made as much base potion as he could with the Nether wart Colonel M had given him. Then, he added rabbit's foot, sugar, and various spider eyes to achieve distinct leaping, speed, poison, and weakness elixirs. He begged Stormie for some precious gunpowder to make splash bombs.

Stormie sighed with pleasure as she crafted and stacked blocks of TNT. "Just like old times," she said to Frida, who sat nearby fletching arrows. Little by little, the famed adventurer and artillery specialist was amassing the components for TNT and a cannon. They would reserve these for their return to combat with Lady Craven and her mobs.

"You're just a simple gal who likes to blow things up," Frida joked. "Remember those fireworks you set off for us out in Bryce Mesa?"

Stormie recalled the display that had commemorated their first big victory over the griefer army. "Those were the days. Now TNT's a luxury. Say, Captain," she said, and Rob looked up from the arrow he was fumbling with. "I'd really like a stronghold to store my cannon parts and TNT when we ride off. No sense taking those with us and risking their loss."

"De Vries?" Rob invited the builder to assume the chore.

"You bet!" He removed some iron bars from his inventory and paused in crafting armor to attend to the more appetizing job.

The burgeoning supply of weaponry gave the cavalry enough firepower to spend on mob target practice that evening. Rob ordered the troops out into the open with just some dirt chunks to use as bunkers for cover. He had them follow Turner's lead in engaging the enemy—zombies and skeletons that spawned singly and in agitated bunches in the darkness.

Turner zigzagged across the grassy savanna, crouching here, slashing there, and taking out mobsters one or two at a time without getting hit himself. The others practiced and avoided significant damage, except for Crash and De Vries, who suffered some serious hits from baby zombies that they thought were too cute to attack. The light of the half moon, however, was not enough to facilitate sighting for the judge, who grazed the captain's ear with a bad sword thrust. Stormie grabbed the poor marksman just in the nick of time to pull him from the range of a trio of skeletons that were acting much like a wolf pack in their tactics. While one advanced, the other two split up and circled around behind their victim, trying to surround him.

Crash recognized this approach and signaled her brother. They donned their wolf skins and gave chase, not letting up until the skeletons were nothing more than a pile of bones—which they then collected and buried out near the horse corral.

"Nice one!" Jools complimented the pair after they reverted to human form. "You gave those skellies what-for."

"Sorta makes up for your sharp shootin'," Turner taunted the judge, whose bow he had confiscated.

Judge Tome did not seem preoccupied with his slow learning curve. "*Ulula cum lupis, cum quibus cupis,*" he recited, then translated: "He who keeps company with wolves will soon learn to howl."

*

The time came for A Squadron to begin collecting Bluedog's payoffs. Rob insisted on joining them this time. Someone had to manage the packhorse, he said, leaving the others free to take the offensive or defensive, if there was trouble.

Jools saw right through that excuse. "Somebody's got to keep Turner from pinching the profits."

The mercenary recoiled. "That charge was never confirmed," he blustered.

"Right . . . only by a judge and two eyewitnesses," Jools said, turning on his heel and leaving the troopers to saddle their horses.

De Vries had crafted the cart that Rat would pull and the chests that would hold the loot bound for the syndicate boss. Rob harnessed the short-legged buckskin and tacked up Saber while the rest got mounted. Then they moved off in a southeasterly direction, toward a pumpkin patch in the flower forest. Rafe had told them only that the farmer had accepted the syndicate's protection from griefers and owed a portion of the pumpkin harvest. Rob, Frida, and Stormie engaged in speculation about the farmer's loyalties and ability to pay, but Turner did not. As he had counseled, the less they knew about a job, the better.

In familiar formation, the cavalry battalion set out across the savanna—Stormie astride Armor, Frida on Ocelot, and Turner on Duff. Captain Rob brought up the rear, riding Saber and leading little Rat and his cart behind them. A soft rain began to fall as they crossed briefly through the corner of a plains biome, where grass formed an ocean of green waves. Ocelot, Saber, and Rat must have had some training in restraint when it came to a free meal. Stormie and Turner had to play tug-of-war with Armor and Duff, though. The horses could see no reason why they shouldn't grab for grass that tickled their noses as they went by.

Rob trotted his horses up alongside Frida, taking advantage of their time away from the main group to speak to her in confidence. "I'm happy with how the new recruits are working out so far. What's your read on them, Frida?"

She consulted her mental file cabinet for the virtual profiles she kept on everyone she met. These must have been in alphabetical order. "Crash is about as straightforward as you can get," she began. "Mainly because half of what people say is lies—they either lie to protect themselves or lie to make other folks feel better. So Crash basically cuts out the middle man and puts her cards on the table. If you can see her face, you know what she's thinking."

"I'ma play a few hands of poker with her, then," Turner said, eavesdropping.

Stormie reined back to walk Armor beside him. "I'd say it's better to channel her energy than to take advantage of her."

"What about her brother?" Rob asked.

"I get good vibes from De Vries, too," Frida continued.

Stormie agreed. "It's nice to meet a man who builds things up instead of tearing them down," she replied, glaring at Turner.

"Hey. It pays to think the worst until proven otherwise."

In their situation, Frida couldn't argue. "That may be so, Meat. But I like that each of those guys has a useful obsession. It keeps them out of trouble and keeps them from targeting any of our people. There's just one thing that's a little off. . . ."

"What's that?" Rob asked.

"Why would they sign on with us? They seem competent enough to go it alone, especially with their wolf powers."

"Maybe to hide?" Stormie offered.

"Maybe they see it as some sort of dude ranch vacation," Rob surmised.

"I'll bet that De Vries is aimin' to dump his sister on us when he finds a suitable woman for himself," Turner said.

Frida shook her head and looked at Stormie. "I think *you're* on to something. There's some reason they want to be under our wing."

"Same reason we want them as cover?"

"Could be."

Rob wasn't schooled in deception. "Well, why don't we just ask 'em?"

Turner rolled his eyes at Frida. "Newbie here don't know much about poker, does he?"

"We don't want to tip our hand," she explained to Rob. "You've got to be very careful what you say when you're not sure about a player's motives."

"Unless you *want* to die," Turner put in.

The rain fell harder now as the clouds closed in. Frida tugged on a brown leather cap and watched heavy drops bounce off the pommel of Ocelot's saddle into the sea of grass.

"And Judge Tome . . ." she said. "Now *there's* a man who holds his cards close."

"Hiding something?" Rob asked.

"Ain't we all?" Stormie murmured.

Frida wiped her wet face with a fist. "I'm not too worried about him. I have a feeling we'll get to know the judge when he's good and ready."

Just then, Ocelot dropped her shoulder and darted off to the side, nearly unseating the vanguard. The mare skittered a few steps before Frida got her under control and back into line.

"What was that about?" Turner wondered.

The next moment, an ominous rumble carried across the plains.

"Thunder!" Stormie said.

A bright flash ripped across the sky, emphasizing how dark it had become without their notice. Ocelot spun in her tracks an instant before another thunderclap shook the ground. Rob cocked his head, measuring the moments. Then lightning snaked across the sky.

"Did ya see where that hit?" Turner asked, worried.

"Never mind that!" Another lightning bolt flashed, and Rob counted the seconds between it and the next roll of thunder. "It's getting closer!"

*

Sensitive Ocelot had predicted the electrical thunderstorm and reacted to their unprotected location. As the sole high points on the prairie, they were sitting ducks for a strike. In his old life, Rob had come across whole herds of cattle that had died on the range from just such a disaster. He knew that the next few minutes could decide their fate. "We've got to run for cover!"

Stormie had studied the map that Rafe had sent them. "There's a roofed forest to the east . . . this flower forest is closest, though. Dead ahead, Captain."

But the flower forest would hold pockets of trees, big and small, that would still have great odds of inviting a strike. What they wanted was cover of uniform height, Rob thought. Now all of the horses were on edge, fighting their riders. Poor Rat tossed his head high, unable to do anything else to convey his panic, loaded down as he was with cart and chests.

"It's the roofed forest we want," Rob announced. "Run!"

Cavalry protocol was forgotten in the pell-mell race toward the dark, canopied forest. Armor charged ahead, with Ocelot at his shoulder. Frida simply gave the mare her head, while Duff snatched at the bit and took control from his green rider. Rob had the presence of mind to pull his sword and cut Rat's lead rope off at the halter, freeing him to follow the others, cart bouncing as he ran.

With thunder blasting and lightning driving wicked stakes of bright light into the ground around them, it seemed to take forever to reach the roofed forest boundary. At last, they galloped through a sheet of rain and beneath the covering arms of oak trees and giant mushrooms that appeared black in the stormy gloom. Armor, Ocelot, and Saber made it, followed closely by Duff. Their riders reined to a stop, listening for the sound of hooves and the rolling cart, willing Rat to follow his herd mates. Saber let loose a desperate whinny, which must have told the packhorse where they'd gone. The next moment, he pushed into the dark confines, his cart still miraculously in tow.

Wet, shaking, but intact, the horses and riders caught their breaths.

"Look out for spiders!" Frida warned, waving at cobweb curtains that hung from the trees and fully covered some mushrooms.

"That was a close one," Rob said, just as the sound of jittering bones heralded a mob of skeletons that had spawned a few blocks away.

"Sweet mother of Ender pearl!" Turner swore, drawing his bow with one hand and arrows with the other, since Duff was ignoring the reins anyway. The first wave of skeletons was dispatched singlehandedly.

"Troops! Dismount to fight on foot. We'll only get balled up in here."

"Ten-four, Captain," Stormie acknowledged. "You hold them off. We'll take 'em out!"

He had collected Rat so he wouldn't try to run off, but holding the packhorse and Saber both made Rob a prime target, unable to do more than wave his weapon. He watched helplessly as his friends displayed their boldness with sword and bow. When the skeletons grew closer and their aim grew worse, Turner and Stormie shot them with unerring ease. A small band of zombies got Frida's attention, and her old diamond sword cut two of them to ribbons before it broke.

"Turner!" she yelled, and he threw her an iron axe.

She put her family's signature spiral defense move into play, whirling with the drawn axe that sliced through the wall of zombies like a circular saw.

Then Stormie noticed a creeper moving toward them. In the half-light, she could make out an unusual halo of blue particles cloaking the short-fused mobster. "Battalion! *Duck!*"

The creeper had been electrified by a bolt of lightning and wandered into the forest for cover. When it neared Stormie, it started to hiss, blue sparks flying as its body enlarged. The growth sent the creeper into an overhanging cobweb, where it struggled with the resident spider for a moment. This gave the adventurer a few critical seconds to retreat and dive to the ground before the charged creature detonated.

BOOM! The blast pattern showered the players with mushroom chunks and ripped open the tree canopy.

Sunlight broke through the hole in the forest roof. A straggler skeleton looked up and squinted. Then it burst into flame, burned, and sizzled away to nothing. The storm had passed, and sunshine smiled sweetly as though the downpour and skirmish had never happened.

"I don't like rain," Turner grumbled, patting himself down to make sure all his parts were still in place.

"Second that," Stormie said, bending down to pick up bits of zombie flesh, carrots, bones, and the spider's head. She came back to where she'd ground-tied Armor and fed him three carrots. "Good boy," she said sincerely, and then, trying to keep things light, asked, "Now, y'all: Where were we when we were so rudely interrupted?"

"We were about to shake down a farmer for pumpkins," Rob answered, putting a foot in Saber's stirrup and preparing to exit the forest. "That'll be a piece of cake after all this. Battalion Zero: Let's ride!"

*

The horses and riders retraced their steps to the plains border. Even Turner was awed into silence at the sight of lightning-induced craters in the grassy terrain and the shattered pieces of one of the supply chests that Rat had been hauling. Their destination in the flower forest could not have been more welcome, or reached too soon.

The grass gradually receded, making life easier for Armor's and Duff's riders and revealing a carpet of

colorful posies. Here, the oak trees climbed up and
down earthen terraces, and hedges divided the landscape like a maze. Saber wiggled beneath his saddle,
begging Rob for his head. The horse loved to jump,
but Rat's cart and harness dictated that they find alternate routes around the obstacles. At last, they reached
a flatter clearing and an inviting, blue lake.

Stormie spotted a broad swath of orderly crop
rows. "Farm, ho, squadron!"

Upon closer inspection, the visitors saw that the
farm was built on two levels, for double the growth
potential. The lake had been tapped with a long ditch
to irrigate the plots. Movement in a patch of vines
suggested someone was working there, so the group
rode in that direction.

"Hello on the ground!" Stormie called, so as not to
startle the farmer.

An ancient-looking woman peeked out of the
leaves and straightened up, stretching a kink from her
back. "Welcome," she greeted them, waving a hoe.
She wore a wide, orange hat and green coveralls. A
string of pumpkin seeds hung from her neck.

Rob tossed Rat's lead rope to Turner and urged
Saber forward. "We—we're here about the, you
know . . . payment," he said awkwardly, producing
Bluedog's card. He observed the successful garden

operation and sighed softly. At least she could afford the extortionist's fee.

The old farmer gave a wide grin, showing teeth as large as the seeds in her necklace. "Well, isn't that nice?" she said in earnest, dusting off her hands. Then she noticed their soaked skins. "But you're all as wet as hens from that rain. Come on up to the house, and we'll settle accounts."

The troopers eyeballed one another. Frida gave Rob a wordless okay, and he reined Saber behind the woman, whose swift pace belied her age.

"Now that the storm is over, isn't it a lovely day?" she said over her shoulder, leading them toward a whitewashed farmhouse made of dirt blocks. "The tulips are blooming, and the allium are just coming on, you'll notice." She pointed to some flowers that resembled exploding dandelions.

At the house, she waved them toward a small mountain of pumpkins that had been set aside. "I know you're probably in a hurry, and I didn't want you to have to wait for me to pick these. Do you want me to load them in your cart?"

"No, no!" Rob said. "Don't bother. Turner?"

"Oh, sure, let me do the grunt work." He climbed down from Duff and started heaving pumpkins into the chest.

"It's no bother at all," said the old woman, hustling up to help him.

They filled the box that had survived Rat's race with the lightning, and the farmer asked, "Don't you want some more?"

"Oh, no, ma'am," Rob said. "We've just the one chest. That'll be plenty."

She wiped her palms on her coveralls. "Well, that's fine and dandy. I am so grateful for the protection from those horrible griefer people. Do you think it's safe to be out in the open?" She glanced at the horizon.

"We haven't seen any of Lady Craven's gang out this way," Frida reassured her. "But we do have to get back to camp before dark."

"Thank you so much for the harvest. We'll see that Bluedog gets it," Rob said politely.

The woman clucked. "Can't you stop and rest a spell? I've just baked some pie."

"Why, thank you kindly," Turner blurted out. "Don't mind if we do."

Frida cut him a look, and Rob's smile strained as he went along with the private. It wouldn't do to squabble in front of the farmer.

So they tied their horses and went inside the farm kitchen for plates of pumpkin pie, with Turner accepting a second helping. Then they bade the gracious woman good-bye, remounted, and turned back toward the savanna.

"Sheesh," Rob said as they trotted across the plains. "I feel awful taking crops from that nice old lady."

"Especially for the likes of Bluedog," Stormie added.

"Who knows what he's doing with all the loot he collects," Frida said bitterly. He probably wasn't distributing it to the poor villagers in Spike City or Kim's friends back on the sunflower plains, who could all use some extra food.

"Be still my bleeding heart," Turner taunted his sympathetic friends. "Weren't you all fished in. That there farmer looks to be doing just fine. In fact, I swiped a couple extra pies from the windowsill for good measure."

Rob stared at him. Did the man have no shame?

". . . to—er, share with the others, when we get back," Turner lied.

This sent Frida over the edge. "You are the most selfish person on the planet!" Survival was one thing, greed was another. She galloped back to Rat's cart, pulled a torch from her inventory, and crafted a jack-o'-lantern. Then she rode forward and jammed it on Turner's head. "There! Now at least Endermen can stand the sight of you."

CHAPTER 9

BACK AT THEIR SAVANNA CAMP, DE VRIES HAD outdone himself. The pumpkin brigade arrived to find a red carpet stretched between the horse corral and the front door of the cliff dwelling, where torches burned merrily.

"A fella could get used to this," Turner said, turning Duff out with the mule and the rest of the horses and stepping regally onto the carpet.

Stormie nudged Frida. "Just what he needs—an ego boost."

The survivalist frowned. "Captain! Isn't this a little . . . obvious for a hideout?" She took up an edge of the rug and began rolling it up.

"Maybe De Vries just can't help himself," Rob said.

"Well, *you* rein him in!" She handed him the carpet cylinder and marched past him into the house.

Then she stepped back outside, blew out the torches, and went back in.

Doesn't he get it? Frida couldn't believe how careless the commander was—and now Stormie and Turner were becoming just as soft and lazy. Deadly forces were against them; Frida had seen that firsthand. Catering to these tourists was going to get them all killed.

Rowdy voices came from one end of the structure. Everyone was gathering in the common area, so Frida turned in the other direction and walked down the hall. This place had twice as many rooms as the plateau house, and they were twice as large, with multicolored tile on the floors. The bedrooms each had a name-tag on the door, so Frida let herself into her chamber. This time, De Vries had crafted a bed, and Crash had chopped an extra square out of the wall for a brick fireplace. It held a bucket of lava that cast a red-orange glow across the room. There was an easy chair and a cabinet for personal inventory items. None of these wasteful furnishings were as bad as the glass panes set into the exterior wall.

Only an idiot puts windows in a secure shelter! Frida grumbled. Perhaps her first impression of the brother-and-sister building team had been too generous.

Am I losing my touch? Running with the battalion had made her rely on the judgment of others—a dangerous luxury. Frida felt her gut tighten, and a longing for her jungle life swept over her. Had she given up too much for this insane quest? If only she could consult Xanto and her mother, Gisel. They would know what to do. Hungry and tired, Frida tossed her leather cap on the bed and headed for the kitchen to find something to eat.

De Vries had designed a great room to accommodate cooking, crafting, and dining. Mutton roasted in the furnace, and something green bubbled on Jools's brewing stand. Kim was showing Crash how to craft a protective collar for her wolf form, and Stormie had sat down at the long table with a wool canvas and some dyes to paint a landscape scene. Judge Tome snuggled in a corner chair, reading with outstretched arms.

"What's for dinner?" Rob asked as he and Turner came in and sat on either side of Stormie at the dining table.

"Don't you have a nose?" Frida asked sourly, slumping down next to the captain. He ignored her, intrigued by Stormie's painting. The two discussed her inspiration for the artwork more intimately than Frida cared to witness.

Jools soon left his potions, and the rest of the team members put their pastimes aside and assembled to share slabs of mutton and roasted vegetables. Turner grudgingly brought out the pumpkin pies from his inventory for dessert.

"How did the job go?" Kim asked. So, Rob and Stormie related their encounter with the poor, old farmer.

"Enough of this sob story!" Turner complained. "It's business, pure and simple. Can't we talk about something more . . . interesting?"

"I know," said Jools. "Stormie, let's hear about the time you mined your way through the Nether and came out the other side. I heard you didn't even need a portal."

Crash turned to Stormie with admiration in her eyes.

"Wow! How'd you do that?" De Vries asked.

"Well, I just grabbed a diamond pickaxe in either hand and went to work," Stormie said. "Straight down, no turning back."

Rob's jaw went slack. "But how did you fight off mobs?"

Stormie chuckled. "I crafted a mirror out of some glass and gold that I had smelted down and stuck it on my helmet to get a rear view. When I saw a ghast or a magma cube coming my way, I let a pickaxe fly backwards. Never even stopped digging till I came out on the other side of the Overworld."

Frida made a rude sound with her mouth. "That's bogus! Nobody can mine through bedrock, let alone two layers."

"I'd been working out," Stormie insisted.

Rob's mouth hung open so long that a stream of drool pooled on his plate.

Frida jabbed him hard with an elbow. "Don't believe everything you hear, Captain."

"I like a fit woman," Turner said, obviously buying the tall tale. "When it comes to muscle, brains, or luck, I'll take muscle anytime."

"What is that, like Rock-Paper-Scissors?" Jools quipped.

Turner grunted. "Way I play, rock beats scissors *and* paper, if I hit you hard enough with it."

"Guess that's why they call you *Meat*," Frida said, pushing back from the table and walking out.

*

Group life began to wear on Frida through the next day as she rode out behind Stormie and Armor. She could swear the adventurer was taunting her by the way she sat in the saddle—shoulders back in a cocky stance, chest puffed out in front of her.

Turner pushed up from behind, letting Duff get close enough to Ocelot's rump to provoke a warning kick. *Can't he ever lay off?* Frida thought, her appreciation for horses' claim to personal space increasing. She wished she wore iron-rimmed shoes to use on the mercenary when she needed to send a forceful message.

"Hold up, guys," Rob called from behind. He had slowed down as they closed in on the plains coordinates they sought, allowing Saber to dawdle and little Rat to snatch at grass along the way.

"This route seems awfully familiar," he said when they'd caught up. He scanned the terrain ahead, where a darker patch of wavy vegetation indicated a wheat farm. "I think . . . no, I'm sure it's the farmer's place that I passed by with the others. When we saw Precious and her gang run off with his horses, we chased 'em and herded 'em over to our shelter."

"That worked out," Turner said without remorse.

"I've been meaning to repay the man with a few emeralds, but I didn't think we'd be meeting like this."

"Ain't your fault, Captain," Stormie soothed him.

Turner raised his voice. "Will you stop with all the conscience stuff? Don't never feel sorry fer doing business," he lectured them.

"You okayed the job," Frida reminded Rob. "Let's do it."

"Amen, sister," Turner said, clucking to Duff.

They found the farmer in the chicken coop, tossing seeds to his hens from a broken bucket. The bushy-haired man wore a threadbare shirt and pants and limped a bit. He raised a hand in greeting when he saw the squadron ride up.

"We're here for Bluedog's portion of your harvest," Rob said, displaying the extortionist's calling card.

The man looked as though he were about to cry. "I'll have it for you . . . soon. Um, maybe next week. Drought took most of my grain." He dropped his gaze to the ground where the chickens scratched for more seed.

"That ain't the deal!" Turner burst out.

Rob cleared his throat. "We have our orders: two chests stacked full of wheat. That's what we've come for."

The farmer raked a hand through his hair. "I do have that much standing in the field . . . but iffen I give it to you, I'll have nothing left to seed my next crop."

Rob stared at him, obviously struck by his plight.

"That's not our affair," Frida stepped in. "Get to cutting it and stacking it in our wagon."

"Hold on, Corporal." Rob glanced around the farmyard at empty cow pens and a pile of broken tools. "Maybe we can accept something else in trade."

Frida gritted her teeth. "*I don't think so,* Captain. Ledger says wheat."

Stormie smiled with good will. "How about some chickens? We could take those and call it square."

The farmer wrung his hands. "That's all I got to eat."

"Well, then, we'll have to cut your standing crop," Frida said decisively. She pulled her iron sword to encourage him to hand it over.

The man's face and shoulders fell, but he moved off to comply.

"Wait," Rob said, dismounting. "Stand down, Corporal," he ordered.

Frida's eyes went wide. She didn't move.

"I said, stand down!" Rob reached into his saddlebag and retrieved two emeralds. He put a hand on the farmer's shoulder. "Here," he said. "Truth is, we owe you these. We picked up your missing horses a while back, but we needed the animals for transport. I'm real sorry."

Now Frida looked to Turner for help, but he just shook his head and nodded at the captain. The private was already on probation and could fall no further in rank. For once, he had to defer to Rob's command.

Frida slowly put her sword away.

As they prepared to leave, Stormie reached into her supply for a stack of pork chops and tossed them to the unfortunate man.

"You, too?" Frida said between tightly pressed lips. "Do you know how this is going to sit with Bluedog?"

"I'll take that as it comes," Stormie retorted, getting back into Armor's saddle. "Ever'body deserves to survive, don't you think?"

*

The squadron returned with an empty cart and fewer supplies than they'd started out with. They would have to rely on their cut from the next train job to build up the war chest and restock in Spike City.

"Two steps forward, one step back," Turner groused.

"More like three steps back," Frida said. "I am *not* looking forward to telling Bluedog we got skunked."

"That's what commissioned officers is for," Turner pointed out.

The captain called for another round of night target practice, since they'd be breaking camp and facing potential mob spawns on their way back north. The horses' health had been optimized and rations inventoried. There was no excuse for leaving the explorers on the savanna. The three recruits were game to see the ocean, so they'd camp on the cold beach east of town and avoid the worst of the ice plains while Bluedog's drop transpired.

That night, when the moaning, jittering, and skittering arose, Rob paired up troopers and sent Frida and Kim on the first run. They were to alternate covering each other's back and splitting up to double-team the monsters while the others jotted down notes. Frida armed herself to the teeth and went at the wayward mobs with a vengeance.

As Kim backed her, the survivalist knelt and released dozens of volleys of arrows into the skeleton ranks. While they were still busy dying, she rose and tore across the field along the horse corral at a file of shuffling zombies. The mares and stallions stood watching as she held her repaired diamond sword steady as a rudder, simply carving her way down the line, from smallest baby zombie to biggest lumbering oaf.

"Hey, save some for me!" Kim complained as limbs dropped and bodies collapsed in half.

"Split up, troops!" came the command from the watchtower. Frida and Kim stationed themselves on either side of the drill field and rearmed as gangs of skeletons and zombies mushroomed in the center. Huge spiders scuttled among them.

Frida had literally worn out her diamond blade again on a dozen zombies. Now, she grasped a gold axe in one hand and an iron sword in the other. She weaved across the open space, dodging spiders and skeletons' arrows handily and taking out zombies two at a time.

A chicken jockey bounced toward her. *Sh-oop!* She knocked the baby zombie high in the air with her axe, sliced the chicken's legs off, and rearranged the pair—the remainder of the chicken riding the crawling baby zombie . . . for about ten seconds. Frida faded back and lit a TNT block with flint and steel. "Fire in the hole!" she cried, and lobbed it at them, destroying the rest of the nearby skeletons and spiders with the same charge.

The mobs were depleted, but Frida's fury was not. She circled in the grass, searching for more targets and yelling, "You want a piece of me?" No more hostiles dared spawn.

Finally, she felt a hand on her elbow. She jerked away, but the hand grasped her more firmly and began pulling her toward the house. "It's over, Frida," Kim said in a small voice. "You got them all."

Frida shook her head, looked around, and realized they were alone in the night, save for the bewildered horses at the fence.

"Is there something you'd like to talk about?" Kim asked tentatively.

"No!"

Frida stormed back into the cliff house to the cheers and applause from her battalion mates stationed on the watchtower balcony. With no enemies left to battle, Rob ordered the group downstairs to go fetch the useful drops.

"Dang. What got into her?" Stormie wondered.

"Who cares?" Turner bobbed his head in admiration. "She's cute when she's mad."

CHAPTER 10

FRIDA SLIPPED AWAY AT DAWN THE NEXT MORNING to scout out the terrain ahead, which cooled her anger from the previous night slightly. She returned with a likely route in mind. Then the battalion mounted and rode off by threes in squadron formation. De Vries and Crash had recycled their building materials and given Stormie's TNT vault an extra layer of cobblestone. Rob ordered Jools to stow half of their excess supplies and gems there, too, to fund their eventual return to battle with the griefers.

"Tell us some more about your campaign against Lady Craven," De Vries prompted the veterans as they moved off toward the east.

"Yes," said the judge. "The Overworld hasn't had an organized army since the hostiles' pitiful attempt to strike back after the First War."

"Who led the rebels?" Rob asked.

"No one person," Jools answered. "It didn't even rate a full sequel. They called it *War 1.5*. It was all over in a few days."

"But Lady Craven's another story," Stormie said. "She played second-in-line to Dr. Dirt for ages, biding her time until she could assume sole power."

Turner grunted. "I ran into Dirt, his man, Legs, and Lady Craven from time to time when I was boundary hopping. They was taking advantage of late-night travelers by lining the borders with their minions. Got so I was havin' to fight off mobs just to get to my next job."

"So did I," said Stormie and Jools together.

"Me, too," Frida said. She waved at the other troopers. "Once we all met up by accident, we put two and two together. The griefers were clearly out to sweep through the whole Overworld, one boundary at a time."

She recalled the moment when she realized what was going on and resolved to fight back, a drive that had consumed her—and consumed her friends, as well. "Most folks who kept to one or two biomes didn't notice or didn't know what was going on."

Crash pointed to herself and her brother.

"That's us," De Vries said. "I think everybody learned the hard way not to try to cross borders at night. Pretty soon, daytime travel seemed just as uncertain. That's why we were looking for a chaperone."

"I got wind of the trouble by what I didn't see," Judge Tome responded. "Although I'd heard of boundary attacks and pillaging, I wasn't seeing any of the boss griefers in my courtroom. Just the unaffiliated, small-time crooks. I knew somebody big was being protected." He turned to Kim. "What about you, Corporal? How did you get wrapped up in this noble quest?"

"It was . . . personal," she said bitterly. "Dr. Dirt rustled some of my horses and turned them into equine zombies." The horrific affair came sailing back to her. "We attacked the skeleton jockeys without even knowing they were mounted on my herd. By the time we found out"—her voice shrank to a whisper—"it was too late."

"If it weren't for Colonel M," Rob added, "we'd never have been able to save the zombied horses Dr. Dirt left back at Kim's ranch."

"But how do the griefers enlist the hostile mobs?" De Vries asked. "Skeletons and zombies aren't known for their loyalty."

"Enchantments," Stormie supplied.

"Some kind of magic that even I don't comprehend," said Jools. "All I know is, it can be used for good or evil."

Rob spoke up. "That's right. We saw Colonel M use his powers to tame the wither skeletons. They'll do whatever he says. And he managed to undo the zombie curse on Kim's horses. The colonel is a good man."

"What I don't understand," De Vries continued, "is how the hostiles can tell the griefers apart from the rest of us."

Frida knew the answer, but said nothing. The identifying medallion that warded off the mobs lay buried deep in her inventory. If it fell into the wrong hands, there was no telling what might happen.

"Mebbe it's based on handsome," Turner mused. "Not a one in that griefer crowd is as good-lookin' as me. And they just won't leave me alone."

"If that's the case, then we know intelligence isn't a factor," Jools said wryly, then he grew serious again. "There's one thing we do know that works on them, and that's subterfuge."

"Yep," Stormie said. "Frida, here, was able to trick them into thinking she was a griefer type. She pretended to fall in with their gang and managed to lay some traps before our last big battle."

"You know . . ." Jools said, his mental wheels turning, "what we need is someone else who appears innocent enough to get in close. Close enough to help us take Lady Craven out." He turned in his saddle and gave the judge a meaningful stare.

"Don't look at me. Those griefers have powerful magic and no respect for the law."

Jools thought a moment. "But they might not notice a couple of neutral wolves." He glanced at De Vries, who rode next to him on Velvet. The builder turned around and eyed his sister.

Crash whirled her pickaxe atop Roadrunner, causing Nightwind to sidestep out of reach on her right. Kim legged him back into line.

"You don't have to decide right away," Rob said from his post on Saber at the rear. "Think about it."

They rode on, crossing into the cold taiga, where the landscape seemed to chill the conversation. A recent snowfall had coated everything with a sparkling white fairy dust. The low terraces resembled frosted layer cakes, and flowers poked from the ground like sugar-coated lollipops. All the troopers could hear were the crunch of hooves on snowy ice and the sound of Rat's cart wheels bumping over the blocks.

At the edge of the taiga they stopped for a quick snack, then turned northward along the cold beach that their vanguard had scouted. Snow-covered sand stretched across the wide swath in every direction. The air smelled of frost, but not salt water.

Crash got Frida's attention and moved her rein hand up and down like waves.

"We won't see the ocean until we make camp," Frida announced. "This beach narrows down, off toward Spike City. We'll have a waterfront campsite for you folks to explore while we're away on business with Bluedog."

Mentioning the syndicate boss's name set her on edge. How were they going to explain bringing only half of the pumpkins and none of the wheat they'd been sent to collect? More importantly, what would Bluedog do about it?

*

Night was coming on when they finished their long trek up the beach. As Frida had foretold, the wide shore narrowed, and the ice plains spread out from the west. An ocean stretched toward the eastern horizon, its blue waters rapidly deepening to purple-black in the fading light.

"Brings back memories, huh, Newbie?" Turner asked Rob, referring to the cowboy's entrance into the Overworld not so long before.

Frida glanced over her shoulder. The sight of the sea had made Rob halt Saber and Rat. He stared at the water, seemingly paralyzed by his emotions. Frida was sure he couldn't help but recall his fall from the airplane into the waves on his first day. Both she and

Turner had been impressed with his ability to survive and make it to shore near the jungle biome, where Frida had found him—alone, hungry, and vulnerable.

He's come a long way since then, she thought. *But that doesn't make him hardcore.* His handling of their recent jobs showed weakness. If Bluedog or Lady Craven got a taste of that, he and his troops were dead meat. Although his gentleness and caring had once drawn her to him, those very traits now put her and her cavalry mates in danger. How could she change the cowboy's fundamental nature?

"Chop, chop!" Jools called, jarring Frida out of her daydream. "We've got to make shelter before the ice zombies come out."

The surrounding snow and frozen blocks called for another of De Vries's shelter designs, which used the landscape to advantage. Before the others had finished seeing to the horses, Crash had tossed Roadrunner's reins to Frida and begun excavating a glorified igloo.

A snow house may not have felt as secure as those made of more solid blocks, but it was as soundproof. Nobody knew whether mobs roamed the area until the next morning, when the prints of a lone creeper showed that it had wandered off as the players remained warm inside.

At dawn, A Squadron, plus the battalion captain and the packhorse, headed toward the ice plains, leaving the rest of their party to investigate the ocean-front. The riders would skirt the city on their way to the weekly rendezvous with Bluedog and Mad Jack.

Frida had pondered the situation overnight. She wouldn't abandon the task she'd signed on for . . . but she didn't know whether she could trust Rob to conduct himself safely. Not only did they have to make up for the short payload, they had to perform another successful run up and down the extreme hills with the supply train and its talkative driver. Frida appealed to Turner to take the captain aside and lay out the *don't ask, don't tell* rules in his forceful style.

At least, we'll be armed if things get ugly, she thought. The rest of their crew and their supplies would be securely out of sight and maybe out of mind. Frida didn't know how much Rafe had told Bluedog about the battalion's actions, apart from what she'd felt comfortable relaying. Her brother likely had ears all over the city, but perhaps not beyond it. He was a villager, not a griefer, after all.

The meeting with the syndicate boss would be as dicey as their jaunt through the recent thunderstorm. Frida wondered how close lightning would strike.

"Let me do the talking," Turner said to the captain as they approached the boundary between the ice plains and extreme hills. "And put on your tough skin," he instructed. "We need these here jobs."

"We've got to convince Bluedog all over again that we can come through for him," Stormie added.

Took the words right out of my mouth, Frida thought.

The horses seemed to step more carefully and the wheels of Rat's cart to squeak more insistently as they neared Bluedog's Nether portal.

Stormie, riding up front, peered at the foliage lining the edge of the extreme hills. She soon spied the minecart tracks and then the frame of the Nether portal. "There it is!"

Bluedog stood waiting, tapping his blue-and-white striped foot impatiently. Beside him, the box of captive silverfish was hidden under its woolen sheet, like a birdcage covered to help a canary sleep. But Frida could hear the mob clicking and buzzing within, and she cringed.

Bluedog surveyed the cart that Rat had hauled such a long way. He narrowed his already beady eyes. "One chest! Where's the rest?" he demanded.

Rob opened his mouth to answer, but Turner cut him off. "Scattered from here to kingdom come. We had it all loaded and locked down when we run into a lightning storm. Lost all but the one chest."

"So . . . you failed," Bluedog concluded ominously.

Turner didn't falter. "Act o' God." He cocked his head as though daring the extortionist to challenge Fate.

Bluedog's facial stripes turned purple. "I pay you to get around such difficulties."

"We can't control the weather," Rob pointed out.

Frida held her breath.

"That's *your* problem! We had an arrangement." Bluedog pulled the sheet off the cage of silverfish, jolting them awake. The ill-tempered, eight-legged mobsters increased their warning sounds. "If you don't want your lives to end in an endless stream of silverfish," he warned, "you'd better make the next pickup count. I want to see a full herd of cattle here this time next week."

They were to collect payment from a ranch on the far mesa, which gave them seven days to make the lengthy round trip.

"Meanwhile . . ." Bluedog stroked the top of the cage. "I'll dock your wages today by half."

Turner appeared to accept those terms reluctantly. "Where's our advance?"

"There is none! And you won't see a pebble until you get back down that hill with a full minecart." Bluedog thrust his chin in the direction of the tracks. "You can leave that packhorse here as security. Now get going!"

*

"Are you sure it was smart, lying to a crook like that?" Rob said as the horses picked their way up the steep hill.

"*Smart* and *necessary's* two different things," Turner replied.

"It's just that I think honesty is usually the best policy. . . ."

Stormie blew out a breath. "Good grief, Captain! Haven't you ever heard of little white lies?"

"Your goody-two-shoes ways is what got us into this mess in the first place," Turner accused.

"That's just not the kind of Overworld we live in, Rob," Stormie explained gently. "It's the kind of world we *want* . . . but we've all had to put our principles on hold just to stay alive and keep fighting for it." She paused. "Look at Turner. His good side's been on hold so long he can barely find it anymore."

"Hey. Fella wants to deal with the likes of Bluedog better hide his sweet, sensitive side. Heck, Cap'n Newbie here's so pure, prob'ly the worst thing he's ever done is enable cheats to teleport farther."

"Cheats to . . . what?"

Frida let them gang up on Rob. She had done her best to educate the one-time cowboy in the ways of Overworld survival. Making it alone, she could do. This working-together group thing was not her specialty. She did know that if you went up against individuals as volatile as Bluedog and Lady Craven, you had to fight fire with fire.

Stormie saw movement on the tracks above them. "Here comes Mad Jack. If you feel a bout of truthfulness coming on, sir, I suggest you keep your mouth shut."

The weathered supply train driver coasted onto the small, flattened ledge with the cart brake on, bringing the conveyance to a crawl. "Salutations," he greeted them in his old-fashioned manner—which Frida believed to be a front for a much sharper edge. "I'm pleased to take up with such able bodyguards. Now I can breathe a little easier."

The riders split up and positioned themselves around the cart for the downward journey, the women beside and the men behind the driver.

"Somebody following you this time?" Frida asked.

"As always," he said. "Never see 'em until they strike." He gestured to the load beneath him—the large chest he was seated on and three more. "They's several parties interested in this booty."

"I can imagine."

Turner appraised the load, fishing for details. "Looks like . . . one, two, three—four villages ransacked this time around."

Mad Jack scratched his belly. "Don't know where it come from, and don't want to know."

Rob could learn a thing or two from this old codger, Frida thought. It paid to listen closely to one's enemies . . . or friends of one's enemies.

"I rarely exercise my curiosity," Mad Jack continued. "When I do, it's to a purpose. That which produces rare stones."

"I admire a man with the right priorities," Turner complimented him.

"Greed makes the Overworld go 'round."

"You can say that again," Stormie said. "I once saw a woman trade her own baby for a creeper head."

"Perhaps you met my ex-wife," Mad Jack quipped, then wheezed a laugh. He increased the brake pressure as the trail dropped off sharply and stepped downward in blocks, past dead spruce trees once more. "Say. Bein' from here and there—as you say you are—mebbe you know the whereabouts of some associates of mine. Might be I owe them a small parcel for a past endeavor."

"Who's that?" Turner asked, perhaps hoping for a cut off the top.

"Brother-and-sister team came out this-a-way. Made quite a name fer themselves in the forest hills biome buildin' fancy houses."

Turner grunted. "What was your truck with 'em?"

"They was fencing high-end goods from a job they was working on. I managed to secure a willing buyer, but I never did see them two again to give 'em their due."

Frida's ears were burning as she listened, trying to sort the truth from the cart driver's story. This sounded too much like their virtuous captain's mentality to be coming from a man who admitted to a corrupt lifestyle.

"We haven't seen anyone like that," Rob piped up, sounding for all the world like a certified fibber. "What're their names, in case we do?"

Mad Jack shook his head deliberately. "Names can be changed, sir. Nope, you'll want to hunt for a blond-haired couple, him tall, her short. She don't say much. He talks with an accent, though I can't quite place it."

"Should be easy to identify," Stormie said evenly. "Can we tell them where to find you?"

"No, no," he said hastily. "Let me know where they might be, next time we meet." After a moment, he added, "I'll surely make it worth your while."

"Of course," Stormie said.

They walked along without talking for a bit. Horses and riders paid special attention to the footing on an area covered with loose gravel. Then Mad Jack began to sing an old tune under his breath, a song about a lonely adventurer looking for a pot of gold.

"That little ditty reminds me of riding the range," Rob said conversationally. "In fact, you'd fit right in there, Mr. Jack. Have you ever done any cow work?"

Frida thought she saw a smug expression flit across the driver's eyes.

"Done ever' kind of work under the sun . . . and under the Overworld, if you get my meaning. Cows, as well. Which range have you rid, if you don't mind my asking?"

"He does mind," Turner said abruptly. But Rob, delighted to talk about his old life, launched into a description of his old horse, Pistol, his old dog, Jip, and his work on the roundup.

"Now that's a place I do not recognize," Mad Jack said mildly. "Where is it you're from?"

"High desert country, out West," Rob answered, exactly as Turner had coached him not to do. "That is, before I dropped into this world. *West* doesn't seem to mean the same thing here."

"And what brings you to this line of work?" Mad Jack prompted him.

Frida could almost hear herself, Stormie, and Turner screaming at their leader to keep it to himself.

"I'm in charge of this battalion," Rob said proudly. "We're arming ourselves to do battle with Lady Craven."

"You don't say."

If a pin had dropped, it would have made a thunderous clatter over the soft scrape of horse hooves, as the other members of A Squadron momentarily lost their voices.

Then, to change the subject, they all began talking at once.

"But that might never—"

"What he means is . . ."

"Lovely weather we're having, ain't it?"

Everyone, Mad Jack and Rob included, knew the damage done. The troopers' true identities had been divulged, as well as their ultimate goal. Those were two very valuable pieces of information—intelligence that would be in great demand.

Frida's head spun with worry. Bluedog would be in the market to buy and sell the news. Legs and Dingo were, no doubt, still looking for whoever might have infiltrated their zombie operation. Worse, Lady Craven and her griefer army would want to finish what they'd started at the Battle of Zombie Hill. At least, when Colonel M had helped the battalion escape to this remote region of the Overworld, nobody knew who they were or what they were trying to do. Now, that anonymity was gone.

Still, the group pretended as though nothing unusual had happened. They met Bluedog at the Nether portal after the last leg of their trip and watched him open the chests and pour the enormous piles of loot into some unseen receptacle. He reserved a few measly blocks of iron and gold ore and lobbed them into Rat's empty cart. Mad Jack said nothing in particular as the three parties agreed to the same rendezvous the following week, with Rob's contingent driving the cattle they were to collect.

Again, the squadron waited until they were out of the other men's earshot before discussing the turn of events.

"I know what you're going to say—" Rob began.

"What part of *shut up* do you not understand?" Turner shouted.

"I promise to stay behind next time."

"Thought you *promised* to play it on the QT this time," Stormie said tersely.

Frida drew a shaky breath, trying to damp down her anger. She liked Rob—maybe even loved him. But he'd just put everything they stood for on the line. *He's not from this world. He doesn't know how easy it is to die,* she mused.

And then, more unkindly, she thought: *maybe I should let him.*

CHAPTER 11

FRIDA'S GUILT OVER HER ANGER AND DOUBTS about Rob caused her to avoid him as they returned to the cold beach and made ready to break camp. It was easy to stay busy. The full battalion spent an hour at target practice, followed by several more hours crafting arrows and repairing weapons.

There could be no slip-ups with the next job. More hands were necessary to collect the herd of cattle from its owner and drive them over three biomes to Blue-dog's Nether portal in the foothills. Because the trip would require several days, they would also need more fire power to survive and safeguard their prize at night. Rob petitioned the recruits to participate, spinning the risky mission as a diversion they might relish.

Judge Tome thought it over. "I always did want to go on a real roundup. I'll do it."

De Vries and Crash were also game to try their hands—or, in Crash's case, pickaxe—at working cows.

No one mentioned Mad Jack's interest in finding the brother and sister. Rob and Jools put their heads together and planned to let them and the judge ride along just as far as the base camp on the mesa plateau. The criminals would not be the wiser.

The crafting session went late into the night, safely indoors in the palatial ice shelter that Crash and De Vries had embellished while A Squadron was gone. Kim took on the special task of crafting lariats from spider string and adding hooks to the saddles to hang them from. Chaos ensued as the troopers tried to lasso each other—a more difficult feat than they had expected. To everyone's surprise, the judge was deft with a rope.

"Might want to study harder at aiming a weapon, then," Turner grumbled. The judge's skill with blade and bow had not improved by much.

Judge Tome pursed his lips. "*Usus magister optimus,* I always say."

Crash cocked her yellow-capped head at him.

"Practice makes perfect, dear."

Rob noticed Frida's uncharacteristic aloofness and tried to draw her into the conversation. "Say, remember when you first tried to help us tame those horses, back before we met Kim? I'll bet you didn't think you'd ever be part of a cattle drive."

Frida had never been on a horse before the day they'd come across Saber and his herd. She had been unable to mount one of the wild animals, let alone stay on and ride it. "Thanks for bringing that up, Captain." She turned her back on him. "Did *you* ever think you'd be commanding a cavalry unit that you sent to their deaths?"

Shock silenced Rob.

"If I remember that last charge right, you got Stormie killed and the rest of us run up a hill to a dead end. All because you wanted to reach the vantage point that you thought would get you home."

Everybody else in the ice-block room froze.

She turned back toward Rob, on a roll now. "Oh, you could've ordered a battle formation across the incline. . . . That would've let us evade the zombies and take cover to fight off Lady Craven's diamond-clad skeletons. But you wanted to go home, instead!" Frida's gaze drilled into Rob's. "If it hadn't been for my bright idea, placing that Nether portal ahead of time, we'd all have been massacred and the Overworld lost for good."

No one had held Rob accountable for the cavalry's bad fortune in that fight, not even Stormie, who had lost her life. But Pandora's box was open, and the accusations kept coming.

"Truth hurts, doesn't it, Newbie? You let a lot of villagers die that day."

Now Turner cast the captain a sidelong glance. He had led the villagers' squadron and felt their loss harder than anyone knew. Stormie sobered at the memory. Kim and Jools thought back to that day and began to wonder if their allegiance had been misplaced.

Frida crossed her arms. "So, my answer is *no*, Rob: I never thought I would live long enough to ever go on a cattle drive. And certainly not one led by you." She waited for a response, but none came. "Permission to be excused, Captain."

The hurt in his eyes made Frida feel a sharp twinge of remorse.

"Permission granted, Corporal."

*

A shaken Battalion Zero left the beach camp the next morning and rode through Spike City once more, to gather food and drop off Rafe's share of their last take. The cut rate did not go over well with him, either.

"Whether you bungled the job or not," he said to Frida, "you still owe me a full emerald. I got you the work in good faith."

Frida regarded her purple-robed brother, whose career as a cleric was nothing more than a front for his black market work. "I don't believe *good* or *faith* are in your skill set, bro. We'll cash you out after this next gig."

The riders left town immediately, attempting to reach their old mesa plateau shelter before the night grew too thick with mobs.

As the sun slipped low in the sky, Turner appeared energized at the prospect of fending off hostiles instead of irate villains for a change. "When night falls, bodies fall," he said almost jauntily. "Say, how'd you like that one, Judge?"

"Somehow, I doubt it translates well in the Latin," Jools murmured.

Due to Judge Tome's poor aim, Rob had him switch positions in line with Crash, putting her rear center and him in the middle of the three rows of three riders. This kept the judge protected when the unearthly groans and nervous bone clacking signaled mobs spawning nearby. The horses had grown so accustomed to successful skirmishing that they simply trotted forward across the icy plains as their riders put up a defense.

In almost rhythmic fashion, Stormie, De Vries, and Jools loaded bows and sent projectiles at oncoming skeletons, whose arrows rarely found purchase. Frida, Turner, Kim, and Rob kept their swords at hand and slashed at any zombies that were swift enough to keep up with the horses. Crash made a game of it, sitting backward in Roadrunner's saddle and chopping at the quicker baby zombies that clutched at the horses' legs like children running for the fender of a moving minecart.

The band arrived at their original rock dwelling. Its caverns still reached into the mountainous hillside, requiring only slight fortification to enclose them safely for the night. Torches placed all around the horse corral ensured a peaceful sleep for the animals.

Frida, however, tossed and turned in her bedroom. She had been awfully hard on the captain at dinner the night before, even though her description of the battle outcome had been accurate. She wasn't one to lie to uphold anyone's image, but saying nothing was not quite lying. *Me and my big mouth.* Only she had known Rob's real motive for advancing up that hill. While he hadn't sworn her to secrecy, she had crossed some invisible line in sharing it with the battalion— especially the new recruits, whose respect he still needed to cultivate.

Then he shouldn't have gambled our lives on his ambition, she argued with herself.

Still, she worried that she might have permanently damaged their relationship. She had never had a friend who was not a sparring partner. She had never wanted one before.

Again, Frida wondered if she was losing her survivalist's edge. And if it was worth keeping sharp. She sighed impatiently and rolled over again next to the bed that De Vries had crafted for her. She was not often given to indecision.

Her thoughts drifted to the incident that had triggered her irritation. Mad Jack had known exactly what he was doing when he loosened Rob's tongue. But . . . the old minecart operator had said something earlier that had been gnawing at the back of Frida's mind. Where had his interest in De Vries and Crash come from? Was his story about stolen building materials even remotely true?

If so, the recruits themselves could not be trusted. If not, someone else might be paying Mad Jack to locate them. Who? And why?

Frida had believed the brother and sister's reason for joining a travel party while still not knowing much about their past. But nobody in the Overworld these days could afford to be fully up front about his or her history. Maybe it was time to learn more about the industrious builder and miner. She decided to pay extra attention to the pair, to see what she could find out. As for Rob . . . well, she'd have to play him by ear.

But the captain would have nothing to do with the vanguard as they set out across the plateau the next day.

"Turner! I'm reinstating your sergeant's stripes. Tell the squadron corporal that her services will no longer be necessary at the war table."

Turner's expression indicated that there was no war table to remove her from.

"If and when the time comes, Sergeant! If and when. That'll be all."

They camped that night in a thicket of small trees on a forest plateau. Crash dug a shelter out of the dirt blocks that decorated the surface of the sandstone. Stormie and Turner whacked a few cows that spawned in the area.

"Might as well eat some beef now," Turner reasoned. "Won't get to munch any of Bluedog's herd."

Frida ate to fill her food bar, despite a lack of appetite.

They traveled all day and into the next in the extensive plateau biome, enjoying the shade trees but little camaraderie. Turner went back to lording it over Jools, who was still a private since he had never sought a promotion.

Jools and De Vries were on the outs, having squabbled over the shelter design the night before. Friction still divided Stormie and Frida, the vanguard sensing that the adventurer was getting too close to Rob. Even the mild-mannered judge's nose was put out of joint at Crash's pantomimed complaint about following the flatulent Norma Jean in the rearranged line.

So, the battalion crossed into the less hilly mesa biome the following day with barely any conversation to pass the time. Crash chopped sullenly at the brown grass at Roadrunner's feet. Turner mumbled to himself. And Frida worried. *This job had better go as planned,* she thought.

But with the captain preoccupied and Jools irritated in general, there was no plan.

*

Rob perked up when he heard the lowing of cattle and saw a haze of dust in the air. Red and white cows clumped together in threes and fours in a pasture dotted with cacti and split by a blue river. The handoff went better than before, as the captain had a bit more practice demanding payment and was now in a good mood, to boot. The rancher had no beef with the cowboy, since they wore the same style of clothing and spoke the same lingo.

In no time, they had exchanged pleasantries along with nine hundred ninety-nine head of cattle.

"Why nine hundred ninety-nine?" Rob asked.

"Maybe he's superstitious?" Stormie offered.

Frida snorted. "Maybe that's as high as he can count."

Rob and Kim demonstrated how to move the beasts along by placing their horses in front or behind them. Frida had to admit that the captain was in his element, urging Saber to and fro, chasing down errant calves, and yelling, "Git up, cow!" to encourage the hesitant ones.

The other troopers followed suit, with varying degrees of success. None of their mounts had moved cattle before, but with a little encouragement, all of them, including the judge's mule, Norma Jean, got the hang of it.

"Jolly good, Judge!" Jools called as the pair drove a cow through a shallow creek. "I'd say she's found her niche."

Judge Tome was grinning ear to ear. "What's best is, these cows make Norma Jean smell like a perfume factory!"

Even Crash had to smile.

The battalion had no alternative but to act together to keep the easily distracted cattle on the straight and narrow. Most of the animals gave in to the herd mentality and kept moving forward. One little steer with a freckled nose, however, insisted on playing the renegade and going the opposite way whenever an obstacle gave him an excuse.

Turner gritted his teeth and sent Duff at the steer's shoulder—left, right, and left again, to no avail.

"Must have some mule in him," the judge observed.

"Allow me!" De Vries called, signaling to his sister.

They ground-tied their horses and shifted into wolf shape. As canines, they were more agile than the horses. As a team, they quickly convinced the unruly steer to buddy up with the rest of the herd and move on. The performance particularly impressed Kim, who filed their technique away for future reference.

The absorbing work gradually unraveled the tension that had built over the previous days. When the cavalry stopped on the mesa prior to nightfall, the atmosphere around the campfire was almost civil.

Rob sighed and licked the chicken grease off his fingers. No one wanted to reduce the herd size or to offend their charges by eating one of their kind. "Grub always tastes better after a day of moving beeves," he said.

"Plural of *beef*," Jools translated for a confused Turner. "And *plural* is defined as more than one."

Turner scowled and held up a fist. "Define this, pal."

Still, everyone could tell he was pleased to be verbally sparring with Jools again.

They prepared to sleep in a simple pit shelter hollowed out of the ground and encircled with fencing so the cattle wouldn't fall in. The captain ordered Crash to guard the troopers on the first evening shift. "I'll play nighthawk and watch over the cattle," Rob said. "It's what I do best. Who wants to cover me against possible mobs?"

Stormie raised a hand. "I will."

The others settled in to rest for a few hours.

Frida had to admit the day had been exhilarating. Ocelot was well suited to anticipating the cattle's darting, turning, and stopping, and was pronounced the most "cowy" of all their horses. Frida had also derived satisfaction from Rob's obvious delight at the familiar exercise, which she watched from afar. At least he could touch that bit of his old life. She knew what it was like to miss home.

A rising moon low on the horizon shone brightly into the shelter. Frida couldn't sleep, so she crawled up the ladder De Vries had placed and climbed out of the pit. She waved at Crash and walked toward the passive herd, thinking to go chat with the cowboy a bit and—perhaps—make up for what she'd said to him back on the cold beach.

Through the muted sounds of contented cattle came the low murmur of voices. Stormie and Rob talked softly from their watch post. Frida was about to call to them when she made out their silhouettes against the butter-yellow moon. Stormie whispered something, and the captain leaned in close to hear. Then they embraced and shared a kiss, fully illuminated by the vibrant moonlight.

Frida's heart stopped. She balled up a fist, backed away, and scuttled off across the mesa before bursting into tears.

CHAPTER 12

FRIDA WAS USED TO SOLITUDE AND THOUGHT SHE was immune to loneliness. But she hadn't realized how feeling apart from a group could enhance that sentiment. The next day, as the nine troopers and nine hundred ninety-nine cows got moving again, Frida learned the true meaning of the term *alone in a crowd.*

She gave Ocelot the initiative in checking wayward cattle and rode along in a blue funk. Days and nights blended into one, until—to Frida's surprise—they had retraced their steps to the old mesa plateau encampment. Everyone, save Frida, looked forward to a relaxing evening there. The drive was just a morning's ride away from the squadron's engagement with Bluedog.

After a dinner of rabbit stew, social hour began around the campfire. Frida had signed up for night-hawk duty and told Kim, who was stacking arrows, to relax for a spell. "Don't worry. I can take care of my back," she promised the horse master.

Turner's lewd patter and the occasional peal of laughter from a distance hit the solitary vanguard like acid rain. For the first time in her life, Frida was not in top form alone at night. A zombie managed to lurch through the cattle, all the way up to her grass block, and swipe a rotten arm at her. Frida fell hard from Ocelot's saddle and could not reach her sword.

"*Uuuuhh . . .*" the zombie wailed, its reflexes too slow to move in on her right away, due to her sudden location change.

Through the sea of cattle, horse, and zombie legs, the vanguard noticed movement at the herd's edge. Then she heard shouts.

A familiar voice cried, "Let's get 'em, boys!"

A TNT charge blew, and instantly nine hundred ninety-nine cattle spooked. As Frida scrabbled on the ground, grabbing for Ocelot's stirrup, their milling became jostling became flat-out running for the horizon.

"Stam-*pede!*" she yelled at the top of her lungs. The announcement was hardly necessary.

Now Frida could see the faces of a few night-riders who yipped and whooped to further stir up the frightened cows, shunting them away from the battalion's camp. *Rustlers!*

The vanguard hauled herself up on Ocelot and made for the campfire. She could hear someone on horseback giving chase. When she reached the rest of the troopers, who were still running for the horse pen, another TNT charge brightened the night.

"Take that as a message from Precious McGee!" came the coarse voice as a woman rode into view. "Done told you I'd be back." She dashed away after the herd, unleashing a long, disdainful cackle, which echoed off the hillside as she disappeared.

The enlisted troopers struggled to saddle their mounts and unsheathe weapons, while their captain just stood there, wooden, staring helplessly after the retreating cattle.

"Stand down, troops," he finally said. "Give it up."

"I'ma go after 'em!" Turner declared, spitting sparks.

"We'll catch up with them, Captain!" Kim promised as she sprang up on Nightwind's back.

"Stop," Rob said dully. "It won't do any good. The last thing a stampede needs is more people running after it." He sat down on the ground with a thud. "It's over."

Frida approached Turner. "What'll we do, Meat?" They both knew this would enrage Bluedog beyond belief.

"Best thing to do is get the heck out of the Overworld."

Stormie overheard them and interrupted. "That'd only put a bounty on our heads. I say we meet up with Bluedog and try to stall him."

Jools broke in. "That ploy will never work. I believe now is the time to follow Captain Rob's lead and tell Bluedog the truth. Swear to make amends. That's the only thing that will save our skins."

After some discussion, the members of Battalion Zero agreed that Jools was right. They would leave the new recruits to defend themselves here at the rock shelter and ride out the next day to deliver the bad news.

"Let me accompany you," Judge Tome surprised them by saying. "My authority might hold some sway."

Crash and De Vries consented to remain in camp by themselves.

"We won't do you any good there," De Vries said. "And we'll be as safe here as anywhere." He interpreted a hand sign from Crash. "We can use the time to add to our ore stores."

"*Our* ore stores?" Rob repeated.

Crash caught her brother's eye again and nodded.

"You know, community property." De Vries grinned. "We've decided to officially join your cavalry."

*

Of course, Frida thought. Now that the battalion had to wrap up its dealings with Bluedog as quickly as possible, the two would-be fugitives were eager to blend in as horse soldiers. They could have just left the unit, but too many people had seen them traversing the mesa. They would do better to stick with the human herd when it returned.

The ride to the Nether portal was grim. There was plenty of blame and hard feelings to go around and more people to share them.

"Nothin' like two jobs for the price of none," carped Turner. "Beggin' the captain's pardon, but you really dropped the ball on this one, Newbie."

As usual, Stormie stepped in. "Take that back, Meat. Nobody could've known Precious was on our tail."

This hit Frida in the gut. *She* should have known. She may have been the designated advance guard, but her training had taught her to check for danger in all directions. Always. She should never have let this . . . temporary setback with Rob cloud her judgment. She flooded with shame.

Stormie continued, "Listen up, y'all. We can point fingers all we want, but that won't change a thing."

Kim chimed in, "We got into this together, and we'll work it out together. Come on, Bat Zero! All for one, right?"

"Somehow, I feel less like a musketeer than a chump right now," Jools murmured.

"Long as you ain't a dead chump, that's the important thing," Turner said. "I reckon we could all 'ave been a mite more . . . alert. I do take back what I said, Captain."

"Apology accepted." Rob turned to the judge, who rode between him and Turner. "Corporal, will you sign a legal affidavit to the effect that the sergeant actually said he was sorry for something?"

Judge Tome grinned.

"Hey, Captain. You made a joke," Frida broke their standoff to point out. "I think we'll need legal proof of that, too, Judge."

And so the air was partially cleared, allowing the intrepid soldiers to focus on the matter at hand.

"Who's gonna break the news to Bluedog?" Turner asked.

"I'll do it," Frida volunteered.

"*I'll* do it," Rob said. "It's my duty. I'll just tell him what happened and that we'll pull the next job for free."

Since no one could be trusted to be more candid than the castaway cowboy, they left the plan at that.

Despite their private imaginings, though, none of them predicted Bluedog's true reaction. The players confronted the syndicate boss at the foot of the Nether portal, the extreme hills rising behind him as though part of his plunder. Rob laid out the details about the rustlers and the direction in which they had last been seen riding. Judge Tome corroborated his story, flashing his UBO ring. The extortionist was not impressed.

"There was nothing we could've done to stop them," Rob told Bluedog. "A TNT charge will spook any herd, and it'd take a hundred players to stop that many cattle."

Bluedog's face was the deepest shade of violet it could get. "Then you must pay! Hand over nine hundred ninety-nine emeralds. Now."

Rob spread his hands. "We haven't got that kind of cash. What we will do is make the next collection free of charge."

Bluedog simpered, "Well, isn't that generous of you." He squinted. "How do I know you'll pull it off this time?"

Rob swallowed hard. "Y-you have my word."

"Not good enough! You'll leave something with me, like that packhorse you used as a deposit last time." He eyed the group, then stomped over to Ocelot and grabbed the reins out of Frida's hands. Caught off guard, she did not expect his straight arm in her side, and he knocked her cleanly from the saddle. He hooked an arm around her neck. "*This* one will stay with me until you make good on our deal."

"Are you sure you want to do that?" Judge Tome asked. "That adds kidnapping to your already extensive rap sheet."

"I'm only . . . detaining her. Bring me six cartloads of hot lava from the volcanic lake on the western taiga, and she's yours. I suggest you get started." He backed away with the horse and trooper, over to the covered silverfish cage. "And I suggest you run."

Bluedog ripped the sheet from the cage and flipped open the door. At least nine hundred ninety-nine angry arthropods shot out toward the mounted members of Battalion Zero, and the band turned tail and ran.

The last thing Frida saw was a cluster of silverfish inches from Saber's rump when Bluedog pulled a wooden axe, grasped the butt end of it, and knocked her out cold.

*

YEARS EARLIER

Little Frida sat in the middle of a dozen young girls, all of them with olive-green skin and short, dark hair, awaiting instructions. One of the goals of Apple Corps was to instill patience in those training for freedom.

After that, the girls would soon learn another lesson firsthand.

"Now, I want you all to choose a partner," Frida's Aunt Lea said. "Pair up, young ones with older ones."

Frida chose a cousin who had always looked out for her at dusk when the mobs spawned. Then Aunt Lea described the drill meant to address trust: The older girl would stand still. Then the younger girl would stand in front of her, eyes closed, and fall backward.

It was simple enough. The trainees positioned themselves and waited to begin. Aunt Lea said, "Now, close your eyes, and . . . fall!"

The first few moments slid by in slow motion. Frida knew her cousin would catch her, so she let gravity take over. Then, as swift as an apple dropping from a tree, the younger girl fell, hitting the ground with a bone-jarring thud.

Cries erupted from the youngsters as not one of them was saved by a partner.

In a few moments, Aunt Lea called for quiet. "Why do you think we did this exercise. Anyone?"

Frida blurted out, "I thought we were supposed to be learning to trust!"

A few of the older girls giggled, and Aunt Lea silenced them. "Not quite. Now, think, Frida. What was the real lesson? The one that will allow you to survive, alone in the jungle?"

Slowly, she replied, "Trust is dangerous. Rely only on yourself."

*

She awakened from the dream and opened her eyes in a large, dim room with an overhead trap door and no windows. The only light came from a small furnace in the corner. The ground was cold, so it was likely ice—packed ice, since the warmth from the furnace was not melting it. Frida's hands and feet were free, but she had trouble moving them. They felt damp, and Frida noticed a small pool of liquid hardening on the ice next to her. *Must've hit me with a potion of weakness,* she thought.

She surveyed her surroundings. Just a bed and whatever was in the smelter. There was no way she'd risk changing her spawn point to this hell hole by sleeping off the ground—or that she'd be sleeping at all. She summoned her strength and crawled over to the furnace. It was busy processing a full stack of stone into cobblestone . . . for what purpose? It could be used for half a dozen different crafting projects, from fortifications to redstone repeaters. Without knowing where she was or who was holding her, Frida couldn't make an informed guess.

She listened. Through the trap door, she could hear a far-off, repetitive sound, like water dripping. She had heard that beat before recently. But where? *Think!* Weakness potions didn't affect the brain.

Then she remembered: Rafe's church! The fountain of melting ice. She was able to cock her head. The sound came from above. She was in the chapel basement.

Now she could make out footsteps and then conversation.

". . . several of them are wanted by Lady Craven," came a muffled male voice.

"I'm sure I can help. What are their names?"

It was Rafe!

The other man spoke more softly or through a filter of some sort. ". . . griefer by the name of Drift. Two outsiders, one Crash and one De Vries."

Somebody was on to Frida and her buddies—or getting very close.

She couldn't make out what was said next; the two men had moved away. Again, above the sound of the forge smelting stone, she heard the fountain upstairs: *Drip! Drip! Drip!*

Suddenly she recognized the approach of footsteps. She scrambled back to her original position as the muted voice said, ". . . Craven will reward you well . . . builders under her spell. . . ."

The trap door was thrown open, and the two men placed and descended a ladder. Frida peeked through the low light and recognized Rafe's dirty, purple robe. The other man's face showed surprise, then triumph.

"It's the griefer! If *Drift* is her real name . . ." The three-legged man blew his large nose on his shirt-sleeve. "That is all I need to know. Keep me posted on the others, Rafe." He shimmied back up the ladder.

Frida felt liquid hit her face. She tasted it, but it was just water. She opened her eyes and feigned difficulty wiping them with her hands, as though still under the potion's influence.

Rafe stood across from her, hands on hips. He gave an ugly grin. "So, sister of mine. Now you know what it's like to be separated from those you love."

The word *love* hung in the air, and Frida knew it described her feelings for Rob first, and for her friends and the horses nearly as much.

"What do you want with me?" she asked fiercely.

"*I?* Want with *you?*" Rafe barked a laugh. "*Nada.* I've wanted nothing to do with the clan since I was dumped at the nearest village as a child. It's what others want with you and your cohorts . . . and what they will pay for it."

"What have we done?"

"Don't pretend you don't know. A 'mercenary collective' my eye! You're a rogue battalion out to unseat the all-powerful griefer army. You might ask your judge friend. . . . That's called treason. You'll die a hundred deaths for it."

"I'll always respawn," she shot back.

"Not if you take enough damage. And Legs will see to that. He's pegged you for the petty griefer who intruded on his zombie slave ring. You must have thrown quite the monkey wrench into that scheme."

"I almost took him down."

"*Almost* doesn't count in this game, sweetheart." He sniggered. "It doesn't count in your relationship with Rob, either. Does it? Or he'd be here for you now."

This tore at Frida's heart like thorns on silk.

"Never mind him. He's nothing to me," she lied. "What do you want with De Vries and Crash? They're just a couple of innocent tourists."

"Ha! I don't care what they are, just what they can do. Those two are the most skilled of all the miners and builders in the Overworld."

"So? This isn't an awards ceremony."

A greedy smile spread over Rafe's face. "They will build me the finest cathedral in any biome!"

"What makes you think they'd work for you?"

"Powerful people owe me. When I hand you and your battalion over to Legs and Lady Craven, they will, shall we say . . . *encourage* your tourists to put their skills to my use."

"And then what?"

"And then I will have no further need for them. They can respawn where they will."

Frida regarded him darkly. "A man of the cloth, killing, extorting, kidnapping . . ."

"I am not bound by oaths," he said.

"Then, what about blood? You wear the family mark!"

Again, he laughed. He pulled his ponytail aside and swiped at the tattoo with the heel of his hand, and it smeared.

"Dye!"

"Yes. A fake. We used it to lure you, and you fell for it." He advanced on her, flicking her between the eyes with a thumb and forefinger. "I am your brother, but have no feeling for you. And you obviously have no love for me."

This was the false sentiment that Frida had sensed but could not identify. *Well, two can play that game.*

"But . . . I trusted you!" Frida jumped to her feet.

He shook a finger at her, mocking her. "Now, now. Love will get you hurt, sister, but trust will get you killed."

"Amen, brother." Casually, Frida dropped a hand to the ground, reaching for something. In one motion, she grabbed the flattened patch of ice and hurled it at Rafe's evil face, where it melted on contact.

Immediately, his body seized up, and his arms and legs lost all power.

Frida jumped for the furnace and removed the bucket of lava that was fueling it. She dumped it on the woolen bed, which burst into flames.

"You shouldn't have trusted *me*, brother!"

Frida scrambled up and out of the basement, pulling up the ladder and dropping the trap door shut behind her. The packed-ice floor and walls wouldn't melt or burn, and the flaming bed would soon extinguish. But Rafe would stay trapped long enough for her to make a getaway.

Frida felt a twinge of fear as she wondered what he and Bluedog had done with Ocelot. Yet, there the horse stood, tied to an ice column, eating some hay that had been dropped on the floor in front of her.

Now the survivalist checked her inventory. Rafe couldn't access her items without killing her. She had only been prevented from using them by the splash potion's effect, which had worn off. Just in case, she dug deep for the griefer pendant and slung it around her neck, tucking it inside her shirt.

Frida glanced around the ice-block room, with its vaulted ceiling and stained-glass windows. *There must be something useful here.* . . . Rafe's computer lay open on a side table. It could be chock full of important information. She snapped it shut and stuffed it in Ocelot's saddlebag.

Her mind raced as she traded the horse's lead rope for a bridle. Rafe and Bluedog had to be in league with Legs and Lady Craven. Rafe might have responded to a virtual wanted poster on the battalion and recognized Frida's tattoo. He could have approached the griefer bosses with a way to bait her and her cavalry mates. Wearing the family tattoo would gain Frida's trust. Then she and her friends could be offered an easy-money job—guarding a minecart that didn't need any protection—to put them in range. Once their identity had been confirmed, Bluedog and Rafe would offer Battalion Zero up to Lady Craven and company. As a reward, the queen of the griefers would make Bluedog rich. She would enslave De Vries and Crash to build a fabulous, new cathedral for Rafe, so he could continue presiding over his church of the black market.

There was just one thing the criminals hadn't counted on: Frida's quick wits . . . and her long-ago training that had taught her never to fully trust anyone, if she wanted to survive.

CHAPTER 13

FRIDA MOUNTED OCELOT, AND THE TWO GALLOPED down the packed-ice main street of the city and out the north town gate. The survivalist reached into her saddlebag for some bread, which she crammed in her mouth as she rode. The mare had just enjoyed a full meal that would allow her to run and jump at top speed over the icy plains for hours on end.

Before they could reach the mesa plateau border, Frida steered the horse south, detouring through the cold taiga until they had bypassed the battalion's camp. She might come back that way, but for now, it was not her destination.

Evening fell, and the moon rose. On and on the horse and rider ran, crossing the hilly plateau until they both slowed from hunger. Only then did Frida jump down and refill their food bars from her inventory. She paid little mind to the zombies that spawned, dispatching them with offhand slashes of her iron sword. Then, she and Ocelot regained the trail and ran on, into the night.

With the dawn, they left the far mesa and crossed the border to a stone beach. Frida reined the mare northward, following the beach past shadowy mountains that held familiar vegetation. They stopped only to sip from streams that rushed down from the foothills and to snack enough to ward off health damage.

On they ran. No mob was fleet enough to catch them.

Frida left her troubled thoughts behind and looked only ahead now, to the heart of the jungle that was her home. All that she knew was born there. All that she had become had flowered from those early years.

The drumming of Ocelot's hooves on stone and the sharp huff of her breath filled Frida's ears. A dark sheen of sweat covered them both in the coastal sun and damp. Still, they did not halt until late in the afternoon, when the survivalist recognized a notch in a tree that towered above all others. She brought the horse down to a trot and swung under the canopy of a distinctive jungle stand of oak trees.

Home, at last.

Suddenly, the breath was knocked out of her, and Ocelot ran right out from between her legs. Everything went dark.

*

There was no telling how much time had passed when Frida returned to consciousness. She heard little girls giggle and felt many hands carrying her limp body. Spots of sunlight fell on her face as they passed beneath holes in the tree cover.

They stopped, and the bearers set Frida gently down in a bower of ferns. A woman approached whom Frida recognized.

"Xanto?"

"It is I." The woman was an elderly reflection of Frida, with thick, dark hair that was wrapped around her waist. Her face held strength and tenderness, insight and wisdom. "Your mother is coming from a temple visit. Why are you here, child?"

"What happened? Someone attacked me."

Xanto held out a gold chain. "Our lookout saw you wearing this." It was the griefer medallion emblazoned with Lady Craven's initials.

"I'm not—"

"I know."

Frida commenced to tell her everything: meeting Rob, forming the cavalry, infiltrating Legs's camp . . . being forced to retreat from Zombie Hill and to take work where they could find it. She told Xanto about Rafe—how he'd betrayed her and how she'd escaped his clutches. "I'm here because I don't know what to do next," she finally admitted.

A hand reached out from behind her and rested on her arm. "You're home now, dear."

"Mami! Then—you heard it all?"

"I didn't want to interrupt you."

Gisel had been summoned on her way back from the jungle temple and rushed to her daughter's side. Two small, wiry girls brought a tray of apples and melons, and the older women shared a meal.

Frida told her mother and Xanto about her fear that she was losing her survival skills . . . or the will to use them.

Gisel looked at Xanto and then back at Frida. "This does not sound like the daughter I know," she said. "We'll have to do something about that."

*

The clan was engaged in practice for Apple Corps. It was time Frida participated in training the younger girls, her mother said. But first, she would have to prove equal to the task. "You'll run through three challenges, each one more difficult than the last."

"And if I pass?"

"You'll be that much stronger."

"And . . . if I fail?"

"You'll have to reconcile that with yourself."

As soon as she was rested, they began with a routine Frida remembered from her youth. Attended by several olive-green-skinned girls, they walked to an oak thicket where the trees were heavy with fruit. Frida was given a long bow and a stack of arrows and instructed to lie on her back on the ground.

When Xanto gave the signal, the girls began running back and forth in front of Frida. Sighting from the ground, she was to shoot at the hanging fruit in between the live, moving targets—with the goal of hitting apples, not runners. As a girl of eight or nine, Frida had been terrified to act as a human obstacle. As a young woman now, she felt the immense burden of shooting well enough to avoid the little girls.

Gisel and a few older girls stood by with restoration potions, in case anyone did suffer damage. This first-aid necessity only increased the pressure on Frida to perform—not just well, but perfectly. Then Xanto lifted her hand, paused . . . and dropped it to her side.

Five little ones scampered across Frida's field of vision. She fitted an arrow to her bow, lifted it, and sighted through them, not releasing the bowstring yet. She knew that when faced with a moving impediment, focusing on the real target was critical. She chose the apple she would fire at and locked her sights on it. She took one, two, three, four steady breaths

in and out, studying her target, nearly becoming the
apple. Then, she stopped breathing and let go the
bow's string, releasing the arrow: *th-oop!*

Thud! The fruit fell to the ground with a decisive
bump, as though surrendering to Frida's power.

Again and again, she sighted, paused, and shot,
never winging a child. Finally, she ran out of arrows
but remained so intent that Gisel had to pull her from
the ground before she realized the session was over.

"You have done well. Almost as well as I did at
your age," Gisel said.

"Almost? But I hit every apple, and I missed every
girl."

Gisel smiled. "I got extra credit. When all was said
and done, we found that I had also taken out a mob
of skeletons that had spawned in the low light on the
other side of the trees."

"I'd like to see that," Frida said with admiration.
"Why don't you give it a try now?"

Her mother declined. "My eyes are too old," she
murmured.

But she still possesses the aim in her heart, Frida
thought. Maybe successful marksmanship was more
than just hand–eye coordination. If you lost some of
those functions, all you had to do was . . .

"Glasses!"

Gisel nodded sheepishly. "I know I need them, but—"

Frida touched her arm. "Not just you. A friend of mine. Now I know why he can't hit a target. His eyes are even older than yours are."

"Thanks."

"I'm just saying . . . I'll pick you both up a pair next time I'm in town to trade. So, Mother, now what?" Frida could hardly wait to move on to the next challenge.

"You can help me with a puzzle that I am having a hard time solving."

"Let's go!"

They set off through the jungle and walked a ways until they reached a moss-covered temple. The three-level structure rose in stair steps that echoed the surrounding junglescape. Gisel and Frida entered on the middle floor and set torches in the gloom.

"Downstairs or upstairs?" Frida asked.

"That is part of the puzzle, and for you to decide," her mother replied, refusing to help with a solution.

If Frida chose the right location and cracked a code, she would open a vault that contained a chest of loot. If she made the wrong selections, she could trigger trip wires that would fire arrows at her from a hidden source. It would be very difficult to avoid taking hits when she did not recognize their trajectory. Frida didn't ask her mother what kind of trouble she had encountered. Whether by magic or by the design of some long-gone inhabitants, the temple treasure was protected—to a point. The genius of the puzzle shield was that each player faced a personal trial and was either rewarded or punished instantly.

Frida set to work, with Gisel at her heels. Torches in hand, they explored downstairs first. The short cobblestone corridor led downward toward several doorways. It was easy to tell when a pressure plate had been engaged—Frida almost felt the *click* that pulled the trip wire. Instead of trying to duck through a random volley of arrows, she tucked her legs under herself and did a back flip, landing where Gisel was waiting in the stone hallway.

Upstairs, Frida opened a door to a chamber that held a likely-looking chest, which was locked up tight. Nothing inside the room appeared to operate the chest lid. Retreating, Frida found a set of three levers on a wall. She could have tried to guess the order in which to pull them. Instead, she thought she could unlock the chest by knowing which mechanism actually held it closed and which might trigger a trap.

From her inventory, she pulled an iron shovel. Excavating into the wall could destroy the levers, so she carefully chipped away at the cobblestone and into the dirt at the base of the walls. This revealed a jumble of circuitry and diodes. Frida studied them and the directions in which they sent the current. The lever that appeared to lead the electricity away from the treasure room was crossed off her list. The other two levers would be the ones that activated the lock.

Now, Frida could use a less haphazard trial and error to solve the puzzle. As her mother watched, Frida spent less than a minute flipping the two levers and ducking around the corner to check the lid of the chest. Soon, it sprang open.

"Aha!" exclaimed Gisel.

Frida beamed. "There you go, Mami." She gestured at the treasure chest.

"No, no. The prize is yours to keep."

Inside was a pile of valuables—gold ingots, emeralds, lapis, and more. *Wait till Rob sees this!* Frida thought. The riches would double the battalion's war budget.

Gisel helped her stack the most precious items in her inventory, leaving the rest for whoever solved the puzzle next. Frida shut the lid of the chest with satisfaction. Then an idea occurred to her. This same puzzle trap might come in handy in a battle against griefers who knew little about the jungle. She would return later on to mine the temple for its redstone and assorted gadgets. Whoever found the chest in the future would be glad if she deactivated the arrow-firing repeater.

The day had been long and full of mental and physical tests, and night was coming on. Perhaps the third challenge would wait until the next day.

But as mother and daughter returned to camp along the jungle path, Gisel squeezed Frida's shoulder. "And now, your most demanding challenge yet."

Frida's stomach muscles tightened. She hadn't slept for days and had taken only minimal rest after being battered, first by Bluedog and then by her own jungle relatives when mistaken for a griefer. She was not at her sharpest. But life went on . . . unless her strength gave out.

*

The final test proposed by Xanto was something that only the most advanced survivalists would even try. Frida was to surrender her inventory and move through the dark to some distant jungle coordinates known as a literal minefield of spawn eggs. All she had to do was spend the night and stay alive.

As these instructions were laid out, Frida felt fear rise inside to choke her. She had been low on resources before but never without a weapon of any kind. And she was so tired.

I can't do this! I'll never make it. . . . How she wished that Rob and the rest of her friends were there to protect each other.

She realized that this was the same situation that the cowboy had faced on his first night in the Overworld, before they had met. Rob had warded off a creeper and a zombie mob, with no knowledge of the terrain or the extent of the monsters' powers. He had fashioned both shelter and weapon out of sand, his only resource. Again, Frida admired his bravery and cunning. If he could do it, so could she.

It wouldn't do to enable cheats to get through this night. The griefer medallion and the rest of Frida's supplies were placed safely in a chest in Xanto's shelter. Then the old sage and Gisel hugged their long-lost family member and sent her, alone, out into the deadliest zone in the biome.

Frida felt oddly light-hearted as she moved silently toward the agreed coordinates to start her survival exercise. Relying only upon herself brought back the balance of control and vulnerability she knew so well. She had missed it. She pushed aside the haunting memory of the mistake she'd made during her freedom test and tuned her senses to the jungle.

Removing her shoes, she felt the cool earth buckle beneath her feet. While her eyes adjusted to the fading light, she sniffed the air. An aroma of dampness accompanied the sound of rushing water. Somewhere nearby was a waterfall, which meant that a precipice might be used as a trap or an escape route. Here, the ground felt firmer and seemed to grow a furry jacket. Moss stone! When wet, it would be as slippery as ice. She fixed the spot in a mental map.

As she had done with Rob on the day they had met, she picked through the jungle gloom for useful items. Melon, cobwebs, and vines were quickly gathered. Then Frida came across a cocoa tree and collected as many of its large pods as she could carry. She whacked at some smaller trees with her fist and put aside the sticks and other items in her empty inventory.

Again, she heard water pouring from a height into a pool in the darkness below. Water had to fall from somewhere, so Frida crept in an ever-widening circle, seeking its source. She didn't want to tumble off a ledge. She found a small river that had formed a pond in a natural stone bowl. Just the place for some night fishing.

Frida crafted a rod from her sticks and cobweb string and tried her luck. She was reeling in her third fish when she heard a twig break. Before she could turn toward the sound, she felt, and then heard, a splash. Liquid dripped down her neck. An odor of mold spread in the air.

"Ow!" Her health bar diminished slightly from the harm as she spun around. There stood a wart-nosed witch, retrieving her empty splash potion bottle.

The sorcerer gargled an indecipherable sound and reached for another bottle. She was close enough to touch, so Frida did, grabbing her vile wrist and yanking her into the water, then pushing her head under with her free hand. *I hope she doesn't have an underwater breathing potion!* Even if she did, Frida's determination might have outlasted its effects. The survivalist pressed against the struggling, foul-smelling witch until there was no fight left in her.

Frida's reward was a small supply of spider eye, sugar, and glowstone dust dropped by the witch. With no brewing ability, she kept only the sugar to give to Ocelot and moved on through the underbrush.

Her ears searched so well for sound that Frida recognized the softest padding of a cat's feet in the dirt. The fishing trip would pay off, she realized, as a feline ocelot slinked into view. When it saw her, it sidled up, turning its head to and fro. She tossed the begging cat one of the fish she'd caught, and the animal accepted it and ate. It purred at Frida, basically saying, *I'm yours!* . . . which was a good thing, because a mob of zombies now groaned somewhere behind them.

Frida circled back to the mossy area where she had located the first waterfall, her tame cat now following in her footsteps. The zombies blindly pursued them. Frida splashed some water from the source over the moss stone. Then she stood still and quieted her breathing.

"Uuuuhh . . . ooohhh . . ." The mobsters' groans drowned out the gurgles of the waterfall and the small sounds that the cat made.

Frida had once kept a cat as a pet that had driven her crazy—not because it jumped up or was noisy, like a dog, but because it was so quiet that she had often not noticed it was there and tripped over it. Frida only switched on her super senses when she really needed them.

She put the cat's small, but substantial, body to use now as an organic trip wire. On the zombies lumbered through the dark. Suddenly, they hit the wet moss stone, sliding. As they tried to control their clumsy limbs, one of them tripped over the unseen and unheard cat, falling heavily into its buddies.

"*Ooooooohhhhhhhhh . . .*"

The pack of zombies somersaulted into the waterfall, and the force of the current carried them over a cliff of undetermined height.

". . . uuuuhh—*sploosh! Sploosh! Sploosh!*"

Frida heard them no more.

In the brief break, Frida dismantled her fishing rod and refashioned it into a bow. This proved an excellent forethought. From another direction, the percussion of bone on bone signaled the approach of a skelemob.

"Hide, kitty cat!" she warned her new friend. "This could get serious."

Frida climbed the nearest tree and emptied her inventory of the cocoa pods she'd collected.

The skeletons marched into range, pointing their bows fitted with arrows in all directions but not guessing her location above them. Before they could lock onto it, Frida employed the cocoa pods as substitutes for arrows.

T-wang! Sh-ang! Thop! Thop! Thop!

The sharp-edged pods were as good as arrows when propelled by the bowstring from this height.

In no time, the ground was littered with bones, and Frida was in the clear. Her ocelot kitty emerged safely, purring.

Then a welcome greeting came from above: a ray of sunlight through the canopy. Night had become day.

Frida knew now that she would never lose the instincts that had been carefully cultivated in her as a child by her wise family. She had not only survived this night of danger—she had triumphed over it.

CHAPTER 14

THERE WAS NO POINT IN STAYING IN THE JUNGLE much longer. The clan would have to do without an extra trainer. Most of Frida's questions had been answered . . . but a few lingered.

After a catnap next to her pet kitty, Frida approached Xanto, who sat watching the little girls spar in a clearing. This brought back vivid memories of Frida's younger days. Had she forgotten how she'd relied on her sisters and cousins when she was young? They had all learned together.

She mentioned to Xanto her recent frustrations with group life, then waved at the girls in training. "Why does it seem so much harder for me to cooperate now than it was when I was their age?"

The old sage sighed. "Everything grows more complicated as the days pass, and it does for each person that you meet. So, of course, your dealings with adults will be more . . . intricate. But they will also be that much more satisfying."

Frida related her doubts about the mission to defend the Overworld from the griefer army. It had seemed a vital pursuit at first. After several setbacks, though, she had longed for her old solitary jungle existence. "But with the state of the world, even that seems kind of . . . well, selfish."

Xanto nodded. "Our way of life has its dignity but also its shortcomings. If you seek my blessing, then you shall have it. Go. Rescue the Overworld from those who would take too much from those who have little." She smiled. "Perhaps one day you will return to assume my place."

"Oh, I could never—"

Xanto hushed her. "Someone must."

Now Frida raised a question that had bubbled up in her from time to time, especially since she had crossed paths with her brother Rafe. "Xanto, why are the boys in our clan sent away?"

For a moment, shouts and laughs erupted over one of the sparring matches.

Xanto's eyes left Frida's and returned to the young warriors. "How else would the girls learn to survive on their own? Sooner or later, we must all care for ourselves." She clucked her tongue. "Many boys are strong enough to get by without any special training. If they were here, they would overshadow the girls. We send them away to the men's camp across the biome, or to one of several villages where they might be of use."

The boys' relocation seemed to be their version of a freedom test. It was up to them to decide what to make of their lives. Rafe had chosen a less virtuous path. Frida hoped someday to meet another brother who had done more with his skills.

She hugged the elder and took her leave, the tame cat pattering behind her.

Frida found Gisel crafting arrows in her shelter.

"Mother, I'm going back to the battalion. But first, I need your advice. . . ."

Gisel stopped her before she could say more. "Frida, dear. If you rode all this way with one thought on your mind, you already know what you must do." She embraced her daughter, then continued. "For your own good, the clan trained you to resist trust in human nature." Gisel's eyes twinkled. "We never said anything about love."

*

After giving her tamed kitty to a small girl who delighted in the friendly pet, Frida saddled Ocelot.

Then, off the survivalist and her trustworthy mare went, moving too fast for danger to find them.

They passed the spot where they had crossed from the far mesa to the stone beach and continued to gallop southward, toward the western taiga. Frida noted that the griefers still had not begun to claim boundaries on this side of the extreme hills. It reminded her of how life *should* be, with players free to roam, explore, or settle down wherever the spirit moved them.

The spruce forest closed in as Frida combed the taiga for her friends, who would still be busy fulfilling Bluedog's last demand. Although the occasional chickens and cows spawned near the path, there was no time to stop to collect, cook, or eat them. Frida nibbled on some cake that her family had provided, giving Ocelot a few bites, as well. Then they raced on.

The horse twisted and jumped up, down, and around terraces of cold dirt dusted with drifts from a previous snowfall. The trees were so thick that Frida couldn't see very far in any direction. She would have to intercept the battalion based on where Bluedog had sent them. Looking for any sign of a lava lake, Frida finally spied some ore chunks and a full suit of iron armor in the distance, floating above ground level. Sometimes, the heat of a fiery lake created a slight vacuum above itself that drew solid objects.

Pushing through the trees, she witnessed that phenomenon. A bubbling expanse of red-orange lava undulated and popped as random chunks floated by above it. A dark ring of grass and dirt showed where the temperature kept snow from accumulating on the banks. Someone had tunneled into it a ways and opened up an obsidian vein.

Frida dismounted and led Ocelot to the edge of the lake, searching for marks in the bare ground. After following the shore a ways, she spied some footprints and the narrow carvings made by wagon wheels. She counted the sets. They'd been here! . . . and they'd gone.

But Frida could now ride in the direction of the prints, which became obscured by a thin layer of snow as they led away from the lake. She gulped a few breaths more of the crisp air, and she and Ocelot trotted off again swiftly into the trees.

By and by, Frida heard creaking and a man's voice. She called ahead to announce her presence, then sprang off of Ocelot's back and jogged up to where the battalion was slowly proceeding down a cow path.

"Vanguard!" Rob had stopped Saber at the rear of the file and was the first to see her. "You're safe," he said with relief that he did not try to hide.

Rob halted the battalion, and they all gathered around Frida and Ocelot, wondering how she had escaped and where she had been.

Jools gave Frida a two-fingered salute, a broad grin spreading across his face. Stormie and Kim pounded fists with her.

"A couple of us doubled back to try to spring you," Stormie said.

". . . but Bluedog had already taken you away," Kim finished.

Judge Tome reached down from Norma Jean's back to shake Frida's hand. "Glad you could make it, Corporal."

Turner jumped off of Duff and—to Frida's surprise—grabbed her in a bear hug and thumped her on the back a few times. "Thought we'd lost ya, girl."

Frida pushed him to arms' length and studied his face a moment. "Never," she said fiercely.

Now Frida's heart went out to little Rat, the pack-horse, who was harnessed to a wagon coupled to five more carts in succession. They were loaded down with buckets of bubbling lava. "Help me out, Kim," she said and proceeded to undo the harness buckles. "Recycle the carts. We can leave this load right here. Bluedog won't be needing it."

Stormie shot her an eager look. "Did you—?"

Frida held up a hand. "There's no time to talk. Bluedog and Rafe are still alive, but we won't be working for them anymore. We've got to get back to the mesa plateau. Crash and De Vries are on the griefers' most-wanted list. We've got to warn them!"

Rob had dismounted and watched her in a daze that gave away how worried he'd been. When she handed him Rat's lead rope, he put a hand on her shoulder. "Frida, I—"

She cut him off. "Me, too, Captain. Whatever you were going to say." With a quick grin, she motioned for him to give her a leg up onto Ocelot. "Bat Zero," she called happily to the group. "Let's ride!"

The horses and riders cut north, then followed the mesa plateau border eastward, leaving the snowy spruce lands behind them. Indeed, there wasn't time to talk, as the day slipped toward dusk and they were still some distance from their old rock shelter. The players all rode with swords at the ready and were well-prepared for defense when an extraordinarily large mob of zombies blocked their path in a dry creek bed.

"Battalion: ready, charge!" Rob ordered.

By twos, they advanced on the thick mob, the riders in front chopping zombies in half and falling back to let the next two troopers attack. The maneuver worked like a charm, with only Judge Tome suffering a slight wound when he cut himself with his own blade's follow-through. Norma Jean set to braying as though *she'd* been hit, and a familiar odor filled the air.

"You two have really bonded," Kim observed, waving her hand under her nose.

The mounted battalion moved on, outrunning a few spiders and creepers, and reached the plateau camp as the moon made a bid for sovereignty in the sky.

Clattering into camp, Frida yelled for the brother and sister they had left at the shelter. No answer came. The door to the dwelling hung open, and no torches burned from within.

"Where could they have gone off to?" Rob said. "Hunting?"

"Trading in town?" the judge guessed.

"I'm afraid it might not be that simple," Frida murmured.

The troopers bedded down the horses and dug in for the night. Once assembled in the dining and crafting hall, Frida caught them up on her escapade. She revealed the lies her brother had told.

"I knew old Rafe was a scoundrel," Rob said, sitting on one side of Frida at the long table.

Turner, on her other side, nodded agreement. "Man don't even deserve a fake tat."

Kim shuddered when she heard of the false cleric's plot to enslave De Vries and Crash to do his architectural bidding. "Reminds me of what Dr. Dirt did to my horses."

"Mad Jack's story about De Vries and Crash had to be phony," Stormie put in. "I'm sure those two weren't pawning goods. Why would they steal resources? Crash could mine near anything they'd need."

Jools tried to connect the dots. "So, the syndicate is in cahoots with Lady Craven's griefers. Since her army hasn't yet spread south of the extreme hills boundaries, Bluedog was free to take protection money without providing any services. It was pure profit. Meanwhile, he and Rafe acted as conduits for whatever intel they could shovel up and sell to Lady Craven. "

"Then she paid them off with what her people took from the villages they ransacked," Kim added.

Judge Tome considered the legal implications of the threesome's dealings. "Bribery, extortion, theft, human trafficking . . . they stood to lose a lot when Battalion Zero threatened their racket."

Rob rubbed his chin. "It was lucky for Bluedog and Rafe that we surfaced in Spike City. That was the opening they were looking for. After killing Dr. Dirt and escaping from Zombie Hill, Bat Zero was wanted, big time. Information on our whereabouts was worth so much to Lady Craven that Rafe found it easy to convince her he was still an insider of Frida's clan and could use that cover to hand us over."

"He's definitely my brother. But I doubt he could've earned the family mark—disguise or no disguise," the survivalist said. "No man could find our Apple Corps location, let alone infiltrate it."

Rob raised his eyebrows. *"Apple Core?"*

"Corps, with a *PS,"* Frida clarified. "It's our clan's training event. The site changes every year, and it's not released until the day of."

"Sounds like my kinda party," Turner said. "Women everywhere and a chance to display my manly gifts." When Frida glared at him, he added, "My gift for taking out mobs, is all I meant. . . ."

"There's more to it than that," Frida said. She told them about the freedom test that every girl took before getting her tattoo and setting out into the jungle on her own. "Rafe would never have had the guts to face one of Xanto's challenges."

Stormie was impressed. "But you did. I'm sure glad you're on our side."

They caught up on the events immediately after Frida's capture. She mentioned that Legs had appeared in the church basement and also had it in for her—because she'd duped him and Dingo by impersonating a griefer. "That must have put him in the hot seat with Lady Craven."

Frida didn't know what had become of Legs, but she told the others how she had left Rafe in the burning basement when she escaped. "I also managed to nab his computer," she said, and Jools gave her two thumbs up.

Then Frida learned that Kim had saved the battalion from Bluedog's man-eating silverfish.

"Running only makes them madder," Kim informed her. The horse master was a student of animal behavior and knew that the arthropods could outrun a horse on the flat. Their lack of abdominal segments, though, wouldn't allow them any vertical speed. They also couldn't tolerate much light; that was why Bluedog had kept them covered. Sheer numbers was what made them deadly.

"We're lucky to be alive," Rob admitted.

Kim had led the fleeing troops up a sheer cliff, into the sunlight. The silverfish followed, bypassing little Rat, who couldn't pull his cart on the steep terrain. When the tiny mobsters hit the wall, stunned, they baked in the sun, and all expired at once.

"Wish we could say the same for Bluedog," Stormie muttered.

"What about our contract with him?" Judge Tome asked.

"I've officially canceled it," Frida said, and told her cavalry mates about the loot she had acquired from the jungle temple.

This news cheered Turner, who asked for an exact count of the ingots, ores, and gems she had brought back. "Well, it's a start," he said, folding his arms and wrapping his hands around the two biome outlines inked onto his biceps. "But I know how to get more riches than we can ever spend—and take out Bluedog once and for all."

Jools leaned forward. "Hey! I'm the idea man."

Turner gave an evil grin. "Then *you* can craft the plan, Private. All that time ridin' with Mad Jack, I was thinking the real score was right under our noses."

*

Bluedog's arrangement with the griefer army had already made him a wealthy man. He had purposely flashed his loot to the members of A Squadron to lure them into remaining on the job, knowing that sooner or later he would be able to hand them over to Lady Craven for an even larger sum. He had primed Mad Jack to find out what he could about them. And he had disclosed the site of his Nether portal as further bait, thinking to trap them if they came sniffing around there in between minecart runs.

"What he didn't figure," Turner said, "was our ability to move through the Nether safely." He stared at each of the troopers at the table. "I say we take that loot . . . by going underground."

Jools grinned. "He won't expect us to hit him from the other side of the portal. While he waits up there with a cricket bat, we'll be down below, taking him for all he's worth."

The significance dawned on Rob. "With that kind of capital, we can afford to outfit all of us in diamond armor."

"And the horses, too," Kim reminded him.

"It'd put us back on the war map," Stormie said with satisfaction.

Judge Tome cleared his throat. "I wonder, Captain. Would your battalion have use for a legal scholar who can't hit the broad side of a barn?"

Frida cut in. "Judge, I think I can help you change that equation."

But Rob looked concerned. "Even so . . . winning the peace is an awfully risky business, sir."

A fire had ignited in the judge's eyes. "*Si vis pacem, para bellum,* my friends. If you want peace, prepare for war."

CHAPTER 15

Captain Rob had learned enough during his first trip to the Nether to know that planning was the key to surviving and reaching their goal. The following day he called an administrative meeting. "Jools! See what you can learn from Rafe's computer files that might help us. Share any relevant crime data with the judge. Frida, debrief the quartermaster on any remaining resources or intel."

Kim was charged with preparing their mounts for netherrack terrain, while Stormie was focused on mapping the placement of a Nether portal and devising a way to secure as much loot as possible.

"What about me, Captain?" Turner sat back, waiting for his turn at being indispensable. "What'll it be? Trashing ghasts? Squirting blazes? Wiping out wither skeletons?"

"I'm placing you on portal guard duty, Sergeant. With Colonel M's help subduing underworld mobs, we can spare you to provide muscle where we most need it." Rob paused. "I have a feeling that once Bluedog finds out about our little heist, he might throw a tantrum."

Turner socked his palm with his fist a couple of times. "I've been known to kick and scream myself— right after I ram an arrow down a griefer's throat."

"Well, put together a trap of some sort so you won't have to work so hard. We'll also need the highest grade armor you can craft. Some for everyone. Carry on, Sergeant."

Frida sat down with Jools to help him decipher Rafe's computer files. Sure enough, they revealed a trail of evidence that could put him in Overworld prison for a good, long time: lists of farmers and villagers on the syndicate's extortion payroll . . . biome cities slated for attack . . . names and ranks of Lady Craven's underlings and their territories. The two battalion mates even found Rafe's preliminary sketches for the cathedral he planned to force Crash and De Vries to build for him. It had an extensive dungeon system, the better to detain more innocent souls, no doubt. They called Judge Tome over to begin building a case.

Jools opened up his battalion inventory spreadsheet, and he and Frida worked on accounting for her additions to the war chest. When they reached the items she had mined from the jungle temple, Stormie and Turner perked up their ears and wandered over.

"Dispenser, sundry circuit wires, pistons, levers, and redstone blocks," Jools read as he cataloged them.

"Say, Quartermaster," Stormie broke in. "I could use some of that redstone to power a hopper pipe. That'd move as much treasure as we could carry."

"And I could use that there automatic dispenser to trap Bluedog at his portal when he comes lookin' for his loot."

"Good idea, Meat," Frida said. "I was thinking that the circuitry operating the jungle temple puzzle might work for something like that." She described the system that activated the lock on the hidden chest or an arrow launcher, depending on which code was applied.

The specialty items were put to use right away. After Turner and Frida rigged the dispenser and disguised it to resemble Bluedog's chest, Turner went to work on sets of golden armor for each trooper.

"Could use some extra fire protection in the Nether," Frida mentioned, watching her friend turn gold ingots into helmets and chestplates.

"Allow me," Jools offered. "I'll enchant the bloody heck out of that armor." He retrieved the judge's law book from their inventory and paired it with some obsidian they had mined at the lava lake and some of the diamonds Bluedog had paid them. Then he crafted an enchantment table.

It was all coming together. Frida realized that if this plan worked, they would face an immediate need to go into battle. Lady Craven and the Overworld criminal element would be screaming for their heads on platters.

"Rob. We're going to want the rest of our supplies from the vault. And a few things from the village."

"That was my next directive. Kim's got the horses shod and fed. I'll make a run with her to our savanna camp to grab the extra inventory. You and Stormie make a very covert trip to Spike City. Wear disguises, if you can. And get back here as soon as possible."

"Right, boss."

"Oh, and Frida?"

She paused on her way out the door.

"Take care."

*

The survivalist and the adventurer were, once again, on friendly terms. Frida had privately vowed to work with the battalion members and put her personal gripes on hold. War was a more pressing concern. Love might require a very long time to sort out . . . and the fate of the Overworld couldn't wait.

Frida used Turner's jack-o'-lantern as a mask, and Stormie wore the old spider's head that the charged creeper had blown off back in the roofed forest. With these disguises and the Spike City villagers' tendency to keep to themselves, the women enjoyed an uneventful trading spree.

They returned with a clock to automate Stormie's hoppers above ground, and a present for Judge Tome. Frida could hardly wait to give it to him.

When Rob called for target practice, they all tried on their gold armor and stacked arrows next to their weapons. "Frida, Turner: You two sit this one out. Let's start with those who can use more practice."

Frida waved Judge Tome aside and handed him the gift she'd purchased from the librarian. He put on the pair of eyeglasses and tilted his head a few times. Then he took Frida's shoulders in his hands and kissed her soundly on the lips.

When his turn came to skewer the hanging ring with his blade, he ran Norma Jean at it and succeeded three times in a row. The body dummies were summarily executed with his iron sword. And the dirt blocks that Rob tossed in the air as moving targets never had a chance to escape the judge's deftly fired arrows.

Turner watched from the sidelines, giving Judge Tome a very wide berth to escape any errant shots. He could not believe his eyes.

As Jools, Stormie, and Kim cheered, Turner strolled over to Frida, who was taking in the scene with great satisfaction. "What in the wide world of sparring got into him?" Turner wondered.

Judge Tome turned a bespectacled face toward the mercenary and cried, "How's that for some shooting, Meat!"

*

The multitasking accomplished, Battalion Zero made ready for a trip to the Nether. Stormie and Turner built, fortified, and camouflaged a portal a short distance from Bluedog's, on the border between the extreme hills and the ice plains. Then the troopers armored themselves and prepared to lead their horses into the lower dimension.

"We've got to make immediate contact with Colonel M," said Rob. "Vanguard. Can you safely do so on your own?"

Between the enchanted golden armor, Ocelot's swiftness, and Frida's renewed confidence in her own abilities, she knew she could do it. She was glad the captain recognized that a single player could slip through cracks where a group could not. She accepted the mission.

Stormie reminded her of the coordinates to Colonel M's Nether fortress, and Frida stepped into the portal, followed by her horse. Purple particles danced around them, and sound seemed to be both sucked in and blown out of some crazy, unseen pipe organ. Then they were through, and every sensation changed.

Light became less effective, sound more indefinite. Everything a player could touch was either sharper or hotter. And the smell and taste of acrid smoke filled Frida's nose and mouth.

The vanguard didn't wait to adjust to the gloom or the claustrophobic feeling of being sandwiched between layers of bedrock. Ocelot's larger eyeballs used the low glowstone light more efficiently, so Frida mounted, and the pair set off down a netherrack hill leading from the portal to an expanse of saw-toothed bedrock. The mare's sense of direction was also keener than a human's, and Frida quickly found it useful to give Ocelot control.

Up, down, and over the uneven chunks of netherrack they ran, skirting streams of lava that generated before them. They slowed only when they neared a patch of soul sand, and hesitated only as they stood at the edge of a wide lava river, where Ocelot needed an extra nudge before she'd jump.

As they approached the familiar fortress, Frida noticed a ghast lounging above it. The huge, translucent blob with useless legs stared at the approaching horse and rider through red eyes and lazily spit a fireball at them. Frida had plenty of time to draw her

sword and volley it back. The ensuing blast eliminated
the ghast, and the echoing report acted as a knock on
Colonel M's door.

The heavy gate swung open to reveal a colossal
head in the entryway. The colonel had sustained so
much damage at the end of the First War that he had
lost most of his body and was only able to respawn
his head. It was nearly twice the size of a full-grown
woman and lent him quite the commanding presence.

"Private!" he said with obvious pleasure. "What
brings you here?"

"It's corporal now, Colonel. The battalion needs a
quick escort."

She gave him the abbreviated version of their plan.
He deemed it worthy and immediately accompanied
her back to the portal, sailing along behind her and
Ocelot. Where Colonel M went, any mobs that dared
to spawn either submitted to his authority or were
instantly neutralized.

The colonel's reunion with Battalion Zero was also
cut short. The more quickly they accomplished their
task, the sooner they would be able to renew their war
efforts. Still, the old ghost was clearly moved at seeing
his protégé, Rob, his horse, Nightwind, and the other
troopers again.

"You're taking good care of my trusty steed, eh,
Kim?"

"He's taking good care of me," she replied.

"And, who is this?" He nodded at Judge Tome. "I haven't yet had the pleasure."

Rob made the introductions.

"My congratulations, Corporal," the colonel said. "Any man who can win the heart and mind of a mule is a prince among men."

They set off through the netherrack, riding in single file, with little Rat tagging along and the colonel sailing behind them. The band relied on Stormie to locate the below-ground coordinates of Bluedog's Overworld Nether portal. After a few dead ends and some doubling back, they found the spot.

Stormie halted the others and sat on Armor's back, dumbfounded. Frida, Turner, Jools, Kim, Judge Tome, and Rob reined in their mounts at the foot of an immense heap of treasure.

A humongous chest beneath the portal had long since overflowed with gemstones, metal ores, redstone components, weaponry, pumpkins, and other stolen harvests. Clusters of chickens and cows wandered nearby.

Colonel M, not a man who showed surprise often, floated up behind the riders and boomed, "Well, I'll be a creeper's uncle!"

Stormie found her voice. "What a mess!"

It didn't appear that the extortionist ever followed his loot through the portal, or he might have tidied up the cache.

"Those poor animals," Kim murmured as a chicken tottered too close to a rogue blaze and burned up.

Turner shook his head. "I don't condone stealing more loot than a man can handle."

"Let's take some of this off Bluedog's hands, shall we?" suggested Jools. He pulled his computer from Beckett's saddlebag. "And Sergeant . . . I'm taking inventory, starting now."

*

The complex scheme would consume most of the battalion's attention, so Colonel M fell back with Judge Tome to hold off any hostile mobs and discuss the legal state of the Overworld. Kim stood by with the horses and mule on a picket line, making sure that none of them were frightened by whatever might crop up.

Frida lent a hand in placing and wiring the contraptions that would transfer the payload from its dumping ground to the battalion's war chests. Stormie was glad to have crafted more hoppers than she thought she'd need. It would take all five of them to form a pipeline between Bluedog's portal and the one that she and Turner had placed and hidden.

The clock would only function as a conveyor belt on the surface, so once they got the hoppers all put together and powered up, they formed a sort of bucket brigade and began feeding items into the first unit. Jools logged each piece of loot into his spreadsheet as it went by.

After a while, Turner stepped back for a break, his gaze fixed on the flow of treasure. "It's so—bright," he said as diamonds and gold pieces caught the muted light from the glowstone overhead.

Jools was dazzled, as well. "I must say, Turner, at a time like this, I can almost understand your fascination with shiny objects."

Turner cut him a sideways glance. "What're we—friends, then?"

Jools pressed his lips together. "Allies, I should think, is a better description. A good deal more effective than friends."

Once again, Battalion Zero seemed able to move mountains—or at least mountains of loot—when its members acted as one. The steady stream of inventory passed from hopper to hopper until, finally, it was all contained.

The delicate matter of transferring it to their chests in the Overworld—without Bluedog's interference—still remained.

Colonel M knew well the price of war. He was thrilled to have aided the battalion in getting closer to its original goal of Overworld freedom. "Best of luck, Captain," he said to Rob. He turned his massive cheek to Judge Tome. "Bully for you, lending your sword arm to the unit, not to mention your knowledge of the law. As someone once said, a man can't retire his experience. He must use it." He paused. "Use some of it for me, Judge."

Frida caught the note of envy in the colonel's voice as the troopers remounted and rode back up the uneven hill to the Nether portal. At the base of it, she got Rob's attention. "Let me go through ahead. Bluedog or Mad Jack might be nearby. I'll check it out and give you the all-clear."

He agreed, and she got down and led Ocelot back through the gateway between the two world dimensions. Seeing neither crooks nor hostile mobs, she signaled for the cavalry members but couldn't shake off the tension that had only grown stronger the closer they came to completing the job. They would have to stand patiently by for quite some time while the full hoppers delivered their contents above ground.

While Stormie rigged the topmost device with a hopper clock to smooth the transfer, Frida and Turner quickly set up the dispenser trap at Bluedog's now useless portal. When he got there, he would find a dummy box locked with the trick levers and think he'd forgotten to empty a chest into the Nether. This puzzle, however, would have no solution other than pain.

Triggered by a lever and spider-string trip wire, the dispenser would fire several stacks of arrows. If those failed to kill Bluedog, he might still die from embarrassment. Frida had filled the remaining slots with eggs, which, by now, were quite rotten. She would be there to observe the outcome. A trooper had to keep watch until Bluedog showed up, to make sure some innocent didn't walk into the trap. After playing Bluedog's victim once, Frida wanted the chance to turn the tables.

Rob had agreed to this, but insisted on Turner staying with her while the rest of the crew went back to camp. Kim reharnessed Rat to the six carts, and she, Stormie, Jools, Turner, and Judge Tome set out to escort the valuables to the plateau.

Frida and Turner shrouded their reflective armor with leaves and sat back-to-back, covering every direction with their watchful eyes. Duff and Ocelot were pacified with a pile of grass. But soon after the others had ridden out of sight, an incoming travel party disrupted their privacy. Moving across the mountain terrace were a distinctive blue and white form, and another with three legs . . . and trotting beside them were two silver-brown wolves with black diamonds on their foreheads.

CHAPTER 16

FRIDA AND TURNER WERE FILLED WITH BOTH relief and alarm upon seeing the canine forms of their shape shifter friends approaching. The dispenser trap would not distinguish between friends and foes. Frida had to make a snap decision.

"We can't take a chance, Meat," she whispered. "We'll have to capture those dirtbags alive. Still have that lariat in your inventory?"

He nodded.

"I'll sneak up and knock them out. You tie 'em up."

He nodded again. Then they waited for the pair to near the Nether portal.

". . . mobs are ready at the top of the hill," Legs was saying in his nasal voice as he hustled along next to Bluedog.

"It's too bad Rafe will be caught in the crossfire, but there's plenty more fools where he came from," Bluedog said.

Their talk masked the slight sound of Frida's feet on the hard-packed clay, but the wolves smelled her. She saw the light of recognition in their eyes when they spotted her, and she gave them a look that begged for their silence.

With one motion, she scooped up a sharp rock in each hand and lunged at the two criminals, knocking them in the skulls simultaneously. They dropped to the ground like broken armor. The wolves whined but held their ground.

Hooves thundered, and Turner galloped up on Duff with his lasso in hand. He sprang off and wrapped the rope around both unconscious griefers. "Never could figure out how to work this thing from the saddle," he muttered.

Now the wolves began to shudder and lose definition. In the next seconds, Crash and De Vries stood in their place.

"Are we ever glad to see you," De Vries said. Crash echoed his sentiment by pulling her pickaxe and chopping at the ground. "We couldn't just sit around camp after we heard what happened to you. We 'let' Bluedog tame us and listened in on everything he said."

Turner kicked the motionless man with the toe of his boot. "We just heard him say something about crossfire. They planning a raid?"

Crash pointed uphill in the direction of the mine-cart tracks then back toward Spike City.

Frida eyed Turner. "I'll bet they're sending the zombies down this way."

"Yes!" De Vries confirmed. "We learned that Lady Craven is preparing for a southern sweep, starting with the ice plains biome. That puts Spike City dead in her sights."

"And puts who knows how many good people at risk," Frida concluded. "We've got to let Rafe know!"

Turner frowned. "He ain't hardly what you call *good.*"

Frida took in Crash and De Vries standing side by side. "But he is my brother. Besides, we'll want him and these two slimes to live long enough to see the inside of a prison."

Bluedog and Legs began to stir.

Frida had to think quickly again. "Where're your horses?" she asked Crash, who pointed away toward the hillside.

"We built them a lovely stable, hidden from view," De Vries explained.

Frida glanced around the portal area. "We'll have to make a stand here to intercept the mobs. You two stay here and dig us a bunker. I'll take the prisoners with me to Spike City and warn Rafe." She collected Duff's reins and handed them to Turner. "Meat, you light out for camp and rally the troops. Bring the TNT and all the other fire power we've got. We'll meet up by dusk."

Turner hesitated. "Ya know, Corporal, I outrank you. I should be giving the orders here."

Frida sighed. Male egos were so fragile. "All right, Sergeant. You make the call."

"Right. Your plan ain't half bad. Let's go with it. I'ma head west and alert the captain. You two"—he nodded at Crash and De Vries—"work on that bunker, and stay out of sight if any more griefers show. We'll all meet back here ASAP." He stepped into the stirrup of Duff's saddle and wheeled his horse to the west.

Crash ran for the hillside and brought Velvet and Roadrunner. She cut both free ends off the lariat with her pickaxe and bound the waking crooks' hands, then asked her brother for help unraveling the rest of the rope and shoving the two men up on the horses. Bluedog and Legs babbled complaints, which Frida ignored. Taking the mounts' lead ropes, she jumped up on Ocelot's back and rode for the ice plains village.

The cleric was not at the chapel when the three horses trotted up. Frida let them all inside, dropped

Ocelot's reins, and led the other two animals over to the basement entrance.

"What do you think you're doing?" Legs cried as she butted him in the side. He fell heavily onto the packed-ice floor.

"Wait," Bluedog begged. "If you let us go, I'll give you as many emeralds as you want."

Frida took great pleasure in knocking him out of the saddle, as well, seeing no reason to reply. She opened the trap door and pushed the two malcontents into the hold. Then she retreated to the center of the main hall to wait for Rafe.

The survivalist had overcome her initial anger at her brother's betrayal. Before talking with Xanto, she had considered his bitterness at being segregated from the family somewhat justified. But now, she saw that the practice of separating the boys from the warrior women benefited both groups. It made the women stronger, and it gave the men free will to choose how best to use their personal gifts. She thought Rafe still had a chance to redeem himself . . . after he got out of prison.

Frida listened to the ice font dripping over its redstone heat source until she heard footsteps on the frozen floor. She rose and waited in the center of the hall.

The dishonest priest entered through the vestibule carrying a small bundle. He was surprised to see her.

"You! But how—?"

"...did I avoid capture again? Your friends Legs and Bluedog are playing checkers down in the basement."

Rafe leapt for the entrance, but Frida blocked his path, drawing her iron sword. "You can join them, if you like."

He stopped and backed away, tripping over the hem of his purple robe.

"Or you can do as I say and look forward to a nice, comfy stay in a locked cell. The choice is yours. Just as it was when the clan sent you to the villagers."

"Threw me out in the cold, you mean," he said bitterly.

Frida shook her head. "We all were free to make our own ways, brother. You chose a dark path."

"Which brought me friends in high places."

"Ha!" Frida advanced on him with the drawn blade. "Your Lady Craven is about to give you up in exchange for taking another Overworld boundary— and the whole population of Spike City, too. Your . . . *friends* downstairs were prepared to let you die."

This news pooled like spilled milk. "You lie! The boss is sending Legs and Bluedog to shake down the inhabitants for their goods, yes. But she won't attack the city. And certainly not my safe house."

"You misplace your trust, Rafe. And that's something Mother taught us never to do." Frida rushed at him and knocked him down. He dropped his bundle and scrabbled for it, but she kicked it away.

"Be careful with that! It's—"

She grabbed it, and feeling a glass bottle through the woolen wrap, tossed it at him.

"—poison!"

The bottle broke, dousing Rafe with the contents and dealing him major health damage. His heart bar was likely low already; Frida had a feeling he didn't eat right or work out much. While he writhed a bit, she drew her lariat from her inventory and wrapped him up tight.

"You say I have no love for you, but you're wrong, Rafe. You don't deserve love, but you are my flesh and blood. You'll stay here until my friends and I liberate this city from the mobs Lady Craven is sending down from the hills."

She reached into her inventory again. "This will keep you safe from them. After that, you're on your own." She hung the griefer medallion around his neck. "I expect a UBO posse will come gunning for you before long." She moved over and collected the horses, pulling herself up into Ocelot's saddle. "Good-bye, brother. And good luck."

*

When she returned to the portal site, Crash and De Vries were still hard at work. They had carved a bunker in the clay and fortified its top with cobblestone. Then, they'd taken the initiative to dig multiple pit traps among the scattered dry spruce trees dotting the hillside. Crash was busy spreading gravel above one of them. De Vries spied Frida and came down to help with the horses.

"Did you get Bluedog and Legs squared away?" he asked.

She told him how Bluedog tried to secure his freedom with a bribe.

"Now that really breaks my clog," the builder complained. "Those two wouldn't even throw us a bone after they thought we were tame. It's the people who have the most that'll act like they've got nothing to spare—until they want something more for themselves."

"I'd say you hit the nail on the head with that," Frida agreed. Then she asked how she could help him and his sister finish work on the fortifications. They led the horses to safety and continued preparing the site for war.

While Frida altered the dispenser trap configuration to fire manually, she added up the new intelligence. Rafe had been a pawn in everybody's scheme. The criminal middleman was just a cog in the larger wheel set to roll over every Overworld boundary until Lady Craven controlled it all.

Who knew whether the griefer queen meant to bulldoze Legs and Bluedog, as well. Or perhaps they intended to escape through their Nether portal, along with their riches.

Hmm . . . that plan might work for the battalion, instead. They would need some way to secure their resources during the fight. Frida left the dispenser to visit their hidden portal. The hoppers were still in place. All they had to do was reverse the direction that their contents traveled.

Frida knew the portal might also be a crucial escape hatch to the Nether, if the battle went south. This scenario was way too familiar. But the Zombie Hill attack had been lost due to the captain's error . . . and she was pretty sure he'd never let that happen again, even if an airplane bound for his ranch in the other world landed right in front of them.

That was the difference between Rob and Rafe. The cowboy had enough humility to learn from his mistakes. The cleric—at least so far—did not.

The sun crawled across the sky and hit the western tree line. It was beginning to sink farther when the backup troops rode in. Frida helped Kim untack the horses and mule and get them settled in their hillside stable to rest. They might be pressed into service again. It was going to be long night.

Kim gave Frida some sugar to distribute. She paused at Ocelot's stall to stroke the mare's neck as she munched her treat. They had rarely been apart since

Kim had first paired them up. Ocelot had carried Frida safely through battle and through the Nether, and had waited patiently when she'd been held captive. The survivalist realized she had gradually relied more and more on the horse's steadfast willingness as she fought to survive, stay free, and try to help the rest of the Overworld's citizens do the same.

"Say, Kim. You've done so much to bring us all together with the horses. We couldn't have come this far without them." Frida meant that both as a warrior and a woman. Before, she'd competed with everyone she'd ever met. This was the type of unconditional friendship she'd been missing all her life.

"It's called bonding," Kim said. "If you're one with your horse, you're stronger than any two separate creatures could ever be."

Frida shot Kim a grateful look. "I won't forget that."

Jools stuck his head in the shallow cave. "Captain wants you both, on the double."

The full battalion gathered on a grassy knoll in between the two Nether portals. Captain Rob addressed his troops.

"Fine work, Vanguard," he said to Frida. "The intel you and Turner gathered has allowed us to prepare for a sneak attack on the griefer army. Lady Craven is poised to sweep into the southern hemisphere to continue her Overworld invasion."

"Won't be a safe hiding place anymore," Stormie pointed out.

"That's why we've got to succeed in advancing and pushing her back to the other side of this mountain." The captain turned to Jools. "We'll have to fight in the dark. Can you provide us with night vision potions?"

Jools nodded. "Already in my brewing inventory."

"Artilleryman? Did you finish crafting that TNT cannon?"

"Negative, Captain. I'm missing a couple parts. But we do have plenty of TNT blocks."

"We can fire them from the dispenser," Frida added, "but we can't guarantee their trajectory. So we can only count on explosives to take out a whole mob at close range."

"Sounds good to me," Turner said.

"I'd rather they didn't get that close," Jools murmured.

Crash waved her pickaxe at the hillside.

"We might break their ranks with our pit traps," De Vries said.

Rob nodded. "They'll be effective. But we have to be ready for long-range and hand-to-hand combat, if necessary." He took in the group. "Anybody who isn't in line with that, raise a hand."

No one did.

"Judge?" Rob prompted.

Judge Tome appeared resolute. He flashed his UBO band. "I've renewed my faith in a free Overworld. Let's do this thing."

"I'm going to swear you in, then." Rob had the three newest recruits rise and pledge loyalty to the battalion and the Overworld. Then he turned to the sergeant at arms. "Turner? Weapons report."

Turner rubbed his hands together. "Already in place: seventeen pit traps with gravel slides. We'll switch out the dispenser arrows for TNT, which Stormie can set off remotely via redstone circuit. Jools'll give you splash potions of healing and harming, and he'll enchant a few weapons with bane of arthropods, in case of more silverfish."

Turner got up and made his way through the troops, handing out gold boots and leggings to complement their chestplates and helmets. "We're gonna look stylin' in matching armor, folks. It ain't diamond, but it's the next best thing." Then he approached Frida. "The battalion thought you should have this."

He gave her a finely crafted, double-plated, double-edged sword. One side was gold, the other diamond. She had never seen anything like it.

"I—don't know what to say."

"Then let the sword do the talking," Kim urged.

"What else have you got, Sergeant?" Rob pressed.

"Thanks to Bluedog's loot, we've got more weaponry than ever before, some of it enchanted: solid and sand blocks for chucking at mobs, short and long bows, stacks and stacks of arrows, and blades of every kind. Anything breaks or you run out of ammo, get back to this supply chest and reload."

Rob cleared his throat. "That leads us to our safety net. If I give the signal to retreat, Battalion . . . head for our Nether portal and wait below for instructions. Kim will bring the horses along."

Stormie raised a finger. "And if someone . . . dies?"

The captain grimaced. "Respawn. You can meet up with what's left of us in the Nether." He rose. "That's it. We assume battle stations at dusk."

The meeting broke up and folks drifted off to finish lingering tasks. Frida followed Stormie to the dispenser to retrofit it.

"I've got to hand it to Captain," Stormie said. "He doesn't back down. This ain't even his fight."

Frida's throat tightened. "You know, Stormie, he once told me that world boundaries didn't matter to him. That we're all just human. He's made it his fight."

"Gal's gotta respect that."

"Well, he . . . cares for you."

Stormie slipped her a glance. "Same as the rest of us."

Frida paused in rearranging the dispenser inventory. "I saw you two kiss one night. I know it's you he wants."

"Not true. That was one of those convenience kisses. You know, like when you go to a party and make a fuss over someone you know you won't see again."

Frida didn't know. But Stormie seemed to mean what she was saying. "Are you going somewhere?"

The adventurer straightened up and stretched her back. "Always, child. Try to, anyway."

Now Frida's heart skipped a beat. She gave Stormie's arm a squeeze. "Then let's free up these borders, huh?"

*

As night fell and the moon considered rising, Battalion Zero's ranks stood for inspection, armored in gold and fortified with night vision potion. Frida's secret knowledge about Stormie and Rob further bolstered her spirits. The captain designated a battle post for each trooper.

The main bunker would hold Frida, Turner, and Rob as its frontguard. Judge Tome, De Vries, and Crash would pull second ranks, after a melee had been initiated. Stormie would stand to post near the TNT dispenser, where De Vries had crafted a stone turret from which she could see the mobs' approach clearly. Jools was stationed near the supply chest, so he could help troopers rearm or regenerate if they were hit. Kim had drawn a roaming position, with orders to safeguard the horses, if necessary.

"Move out!" Rob called in the dwindling light.

They took up battle stations and listened.

Soon the inevitable chorus of the zombies' lament and the skeletons' bony drumbeat rang through the mountains of the extreme hills.

In the bunker, Turner held out a fist. "This is it, ladies and gentlemen!"

Frida and Rob reached out and pounded it.

Night vision gave them a daylight view of waves of zombies stomping their way deliberately down the rocky terraces. Every now and then, one lost a lower limb or simply tripped and cartwheeled down the slope to its death. Frida felt the breath stall in her chest as faster-moving skeletons pushed between their hostile brethren and overtook them, running down the hillside. Both mobs were haphazardly armored with whatever the griefers had managed to steal.

With Legs, Bluedog, and Rafe detained in the city, the battalion enjoyed the element of surprise. Frida wondered who was commanding the legions. Lady Craven had absorbed Dr. Dirt's powers in the last battle, and it was doubtful that he could respawn. Dingo and the lesser griefers would have neither the experience nor the authority to direct the hostile mobs at their bidding.

Nevertheless, the monsters appeared to have their orders. Onward they swept, descending from Zombie Hill toward the biome boundary and the unsuspecting inhabitants of Spike City.

"Uuuuhh . . . ooohhh-*oh-oh!*" The zombies' cries echoed and carried across the foothills and into the plains.

"They're closing in!" Frida said, steeling herself.

"Wait for my orders," Rob reminded the battalion.

Then the first wave of skeletons hit the gravel slides. Frida saw the victims slip, throw back their skulls, and lose grips on their weapons. The sound of bone on bone rose frightfully as they slid into the pits.

Turner fiddled with his bow. "Now, Captain?"

"Wait," Rob said through tight lips.

The zombies directly behind the fallen skeletons could not fight gravity's hold. Mighty moans were unleashed as the pits swallowed dozens of flailing zombies. The unharmed skeletons, though, were able to plant their bony feet and change direction. They avoided the pits as more of their undead counterparts fell in.

When the skelemob leaders were within about sixty blocks, Rob stood up. "Battalion Zero: *Attack!*"

He crouched and aimed his bow at the hillside marauders. He, Frida, and Turner let arrows fly, dealing extra damage from their power-enchanted bows when they hit their marks.

P-twang! Sh-oof! Th-oop! The sound of bowstrings and arrows in action punctuated the bone clacking, groaning, and audible results of bodies hitting gravel and pit trap floors.

"Stormie! Give them a taste of TNT," Rob yelled above the noise.

Now came the fizzle and click of the dispenser's trigger, and all-encompassing explosions filled the night. Half a dozen rounds knocked out random gangs of zombies and skeletons, sending limbs, bones, and bits of armor into the sky. The stench spread.

In the bunker, Frida and company fell back to reload, while the newbies put up a decent offense with their bows—Judge Tome included. Turner scuttled over to Jools at his supply chest and grabbed more stacks of arrows.

Turner clapped the quartermaster on the back. "Hang onto your helmet, pal. It's about to get interesting." Then he dropped to his belly and shimmied back to the bunker.

The cobblestone blind caught most of the arrows sent by the skeletons, but one finally tagged De Vries in the arm as he exposed himself to make a shot. This enraged his sister. She dropped her bow and picked up another one enchanted to ignite ammunition. Then she sent a succession of flaming arrows at a ring of dead spruce trees, engulfing the shooter skeleton and a trio of zombies in a fatal ring of fire. Practice had, indeed, perfected the miner's aim.

The blaze jumped from tree patch to tree patch until a fire line zigzagged halfway across the hill. In the increased light, Frida spotted a cluster of agile bodies picking their way down the cliff. She pointed them out to her battalion mates.

"Do you see what I see?" Stormie called with unwelcome recognition in her voice.

One of the creatures was much more substantial than the rest—and sported a pair of very large wings.

CHAPTER 17

THERE WAS NO TIME TO MOUNT AN OFFENSIVE ON the descending griefers. The mobs must have been reinforced with multiple spawn eggs, for Frida had never seen such a relentless stream of them. With every ten lost to the pit traps, twenty more seemed to spit from the summit onto the moon-shadowed mountain. On and on they swarmed down the extreme hills, diverted from their village target by the intervention of Battalion Zero.

Thirty blocks and closing . . . now the bunker defenders could see the hostiles' black eye holes and smell the zombies' rotting flesh.

"Stormie! Another round!" Rob yelled. It might be their last chance to use the TNT dispenser without putting troopers in the blast zone.

The artilleryman discharged the weapon—once, twice, three times . . . but only the first block ignited. A moment later, both remaining blocks blew, supercharging the air with their explosive power. This knocked Stormie from her turret and jarred the brainpan of every trooper in the bunker as chunks of flesh, bone, and armor rained down on them.

Frida struggled to regain her self-control. From her post at the stable, Kim saw an opening. "Jools!" the horse master cried at the top of her tiny lungs. "Load the dispenser with sand . . . I'll cover you!"

The quartermaster did as the corporal ordered, running from his supply chest just as she galloped Nightwind across the foot of Zombie Hill. Kim held the reins in her right hand and a smite-enchanted sword in her left, locking her elbow and tearing at the nearest line of zombies and skeletons like a letter opener through onion skin. Her golden armor kept their grasping limbs from dealing serious damage. The near-suicidal charge gave Jools enough time to stuff sand blocks into the dispenser and gave Stormie a chance to recover her footing and hit the ignition button.

Kim retreated behind them. Chunks of sand shot in perfect arcs over the bunker and burst upon the approaching mobs, suffocating them in moments. As Stormie had noted, however, the dispenser's aim was less than perfect. Some groaning, clacking monsters escaped hits entirely and now homed in on the battalion mates clustered in the bunker.

Sixteen blocks and closing . . . this short distance rattled the newest recruits and sent Turner into overdrive. He jumped to his feet and taunted their enemies as he fired arrow after arrow, and finally, an enchanted axe, from his long bow.

"Looking for hot water? Don't cry when you get *burned*—"

Sh-oo-oop!

"Want your mommy. . . ?"

Sh-wang!

"Find out who's your *daddy*. . . ."

Th-wack!

Turner's enthusiasm bled over to the rest of the troopers, who rallied to empty their bows . . . and soon did. With walking carcasses closing in from ten blocks away, only splash potions might hold them off.

"Battalion! Bottles at the ready!" Rob shouted.

The bunker mates fumbled for bottles. De Vries and Crash grabbed them first and used their bows to propel the sticky black brews at the mobs.

To everyone's horror, these had no effect. Nine blocks, eight blocks . . .

Frida flashed on the problem. "Wrong potion!" Spells of harming would heal the undead. She scrambled for bottles of red fluid. "Everybody! Toss these . . . *quick!*"

The more experienced players realized the newbies' mistake and lunged for the red potions, hurling them with rapid fire at the looming monsters.

Bam . . . bam . . . BAM!

Healing elixir splashed in a curtain before the bunker, taking down hostiles left and right. Fortunately, the excess drops only aided the troopers' health.

In the relative calm that ensued, a gravelly voice sailed down from the foothills. "Battalion Zero! Give up . . . your time has come!"

*

YEARS EARLIER

Little Frida crept through the underbrush, listening hard for signs of an ambush. Her very first Apple Corps experience could not end in failure. She must achieve the goal: reaching the jungle temple and retrieving the golden apple from its stairway. Inching along the ocelot path, she knew the temple was close but could not see it through the vine-strewn wall of tall trees. She came to a clearing where the path split, disappearing into three different thickets.

Which one—?

She chose the left . . . and the next moment a body popped up in front of her.

"Mother!"

But there was no response. *A loaded dummy!* she realized, moving off to the right.

Another body blocked her way . . . Gisel again. But Frida's call received no reply.

She took the middle path and ran all the way to the moss-covered temple steps. There, shining in a ray of light that had broken through the tree canopy, lay a golden apple. Again, an image of Gisel appeared, at the foot of the stairs.

"Mami?" Frida called uncertainly.

This time, to her intense joy, her mother answered, beckoned, and clasped her hand. Together, they moved toward the golden fruit, and Frida claimed it.

"But . . . what was my lesson?" she asked.

The small girl could not be expected to comprehend it on her own. Gisel said, "Always ask your heart. To trust is not to love. But to love is to trust."

*

Frida tried to guess what the griefer boss's next move would be. Lady Craven could now be seen a good fifty blocks off, distinguished by the set of iron wings that she used for protection, not flight. Wearing them revealed her anticipation of a counterattack forceful enough to inflict damage . . . which meant that she *could* be harmed, after all.

"Captain! She'll be sending her legions to unlock Bluedog's Nether chest. We've taken out so much of the skeletons' weaponry that they need to rearm."

Jools heard her. From his post, he called, "That means our valuables are at risk! We've got to secure the portal."

Rob knew they were right. "Battalion . . . fall back to the portal. Corporal Kim! Bring the horses."

As they scrambled to obey his orders, a new threat crawled with terrifying speed down the hillside.

A file of spider jockeys advanced like a line of fire ants in their direction. The skeletons atop the spiders carried swords, and the arachnids, themselves, might deal doses of poison if they'd been cave spawned.

"Captain!" screamed Kim. "Spiders aren't just arachnids—they're arthropods!"

Turner stopped in his tracks, adding two appropriately enchanted axes from his inventory. "These is my kinda chopsticks," he growled.

Crash tugged at Rob's sleeve, swinging her pick-axe, and the captain nodded. "You two! Hold them off while we get our supplies moving through the portal. Then rejoin the troops at my order." He left Turner and Crash in front of the bunker to meet the oncoming gang of ghouls.

The eight-legged steeds now jumped whole blocks in their haste to close the space between the hillside and the enemy bunker. They jostled their skeleton jockeys in a deafening crunch of bones and clanking of armor—which nearly drowned out the thumping of Frida's heart in her chest. As she made for the battalion's Nether portal, she felt a boost from Turner's defiant voice.

"Hungry little spider? All ya hafta do . . . is *axe!*"

Frida heard the sound of two diamond blades slicing through eight spider legs. Then she glanced over her shoulder to see Crash dealing death blows to two skeletons at a time, swiping first forward, then back, with her lethal pickaxe.

Turner copied the technique, planting himself and swinging his torso to and fro, using his bane-enchanted axes to welcome his victims to the deadly party: "If I knew you was comin', I'd've baked a *cake!*"

In short order, the tactical team of spiders and skeletons was exterminated. Turner and Crash stared at one another, then grinned and crossed their blades in victory. The captain called them back, and they hustled to rejoin the rest of the crew.

Undeterred by the spider jockeys' failure, from a safe distance, Lady Craven announced, "It is you who will be my just desserts, Battalion Zero. . . . Have a taste of *this!*"

Out of a cavern on the hillside poured a flood of zombies—whole families, mutations, disembodied heads, transformed villagers, cursed animals—even little, old lady zombies armed with canes. Frida could scarcely believe the magnitude of the mob . . . and, for a moment, regretted giving her protective medallion away to her no-good brother.

She eyed Stormie, who stood nearby monitoring the hopper clock that was sending their necessaries into the Nether. The talented rebel wanted nothing more than to be free to roam the Overworld on a whim. If she felt overmatched, she might depart at any moment—and Frida wouldn't blame her.

Jools tapped his foot anxiously beside Stormie, ticking off the inventory in his near-photographic memory. The quartermaster had, once upon a time, remained neutral, seeking out profitable conflicts but placing his loyalties on neither side. Rob had convinced him to throw his weight behind the battalion in the last fight . . . but how long would the captain be able to count on that support?

Frida wiped her sweaty brow and acknowledged Turner's shoulder punch as he dashed by, heading toward the ammunition stacks. Her old friend and adversary had, perhaps, the simplest of objectives: making money. While she had often complained about his one-track mind, now she envied him his black and white choices. With the enormous amount of loot transferred to the Nether, he might yet choose riches over solidarity.

The three newest recruits stood to lose the most in this battle, though. They had less invested in the war effort and greater chance of capture or death. Trying to gain experience as one wielded a sword was more likely to result in AFK than XP.

Now Kim approached, leading Saber and trusting the rest of the herd to follow him. They were all saddled, except for little Rat, whose packhorse days might be over. If only Kim could take him back to her ranch in the plains, far on the other side of these mountainous hills. If anyone deserved to be reunited with her equine friends, it was the battalion's horse master.

"Captain! We might be able to outrun those zombies on horseback."

"But—not Beckett." Jools choked on the words.

"Supplies are almost through the hopper, sir," Stormie alerted Rob. "Do you want us to follow?"

They all stared at the hillside, which had become a dark sea of writhing green bodies.

Rob hesitated. Frida knew where he'd rather be . . . and instead, he had taken it upon himself to keep all of them alive—to continue a fight they might not be able to win, for people who couldn't fight for themselves.

She noticed movement in the moonlight, up near the minecart tracks.

They might still have one more chance.

*

Frida spoke to Jools, and they explained their idea to Rob. He agreed with it, but now he had to make a very difficult decision. Seven troopers could not hold off a sea of zombies for long. If they stayed here, and Frida's plan didn't work, Battalion Zero and the people of Spike City might be wiped out. But if Rob sent them to the Nether, and the plan failed, the villagers would definitely die.

Rob had the presence of mind to consult Judge Tome, who was practiced in thoughtful decision making, after all.

The judge glanced over his shoulder and said, "When in doubt, son, take a vote."

It was the quickest unanimous resolution ever reached. They would stay.

"Are you sure, Quartermaster?" Rob asked.

Jools waved him away with his hands. "Go, go! Just make sure you do exactly as I said."

With that, Rob and Frida mounted Saber and Ocelot and turned toward the hillside. The battalion placed all their torches, for both a show of force at the portal and to stave off the mobs as long as possible.

"Go get 'em!" Turner shouted.

Frida and Rob urged their mounts along the western edge of the promontory, with the minecart tracks between them and the parade of zombies. Now she and the captain could clearly see action on the tracks: it was Lady Craven and a couple of guards in the minecart, headed toward the portal sites.

"We've got to intercept them," Frida said.

Rob just grunted, and Saber and Ocelot, with their keen vision, continued their diagonal climb. The trees that had been set on fire earlier gave off eerie wisps of smoke, and the horses picked their way around them. Again, Frida was struck by the mare's reliability in the worst of situations. How had she ever survived without Ocelot?

The horses were gaining ground on the intersection with the minecart, which must have been moving at a preprogrammed speed—slowed for the downhill. When they came within twenty blocks, Rob and Frida drew their bows. A few moments later, they sent warning shots at the cart. Lady Craven unleashed a gritty laugh. They sent more arrows her way, hitting the griefer queen's cohorts but bouncing off her iron wings.

Suddenly, Saber stumbled and fell to his knees, tossing Rob sideways in the saddle. They slid back two blocks, but Rob regained his seat, and Saber struggled to his feet. When the warhorse tried to jump up the blocks, he faltered.

"Frida! It's his bad leg. He's lamed it again. You'll have to go on alone!"

Frida reined Ocelot back to where the horse and rider stood. "I . . . can't, Captain."

"Yes, you can, Corporal. If anyone in this world can stop Lady Craven, it's you." Rob swallowed hard. "I knew it that first day in the jungle—you were the strongest, bravest person I'd ever met."

Frida couldn't help but feel she didn't measure up to that description.

Rob implored her to go. "I . . . have extremely complicated feelings for you, Corporal. But I know what you're capable of. Trust me."

Frida looked at him with tears in her eyes. Then she turned and rode off across the slope.

She did trust him, and she trusted her horse. Riding any other animal at this speed on these rocks would have been sheer madness. They'd lost precious moments . . . but they could still catch up.

The roar of zombies overcame even Lady Craven's construction-site voice, and Frida could not make out what the griefer boss shouted as she approached. The survivalist had never been near enough before to see the woman's chalk-white face, black lips, and emerald-green eyes sticking out of a pair of huge iron wings, which were wrapped tightly around her as a shield.

As Ocelot drew alongside, Frida pulled her sword. She could only hope that blood flowed through the villain's veins.

The sight of the weapon caused Lady Craven's bodyguards to dive out of the cart and take their chances at falling down the steep precipice. But the rigid pair of wings would not allow Lady Craven to exit the high-sided cart.

Frida galloped a few blocks ahead of the slow-moving vehicle, jumped down from Ocelot, and jammed a gold ingot beneath the cart wheels. It ground to a stop, with the thunderstruck griefer still trapped inside. She punched at the computer keypad with long, black fingernails, wildly trying to override the inert program.

The survivalist crawled up and leveled her double-bladed sword at the griefer's throat, looking her in the eye. Lady Craven grabbed for the enchanted medallion that hung around her neck.

"Too late!" Frida hooked the pendant's chain with her blade and flicked it away, into the rocks. The clamor of zombies was fading as the legions rushed down the hill. "Your mobs aren't here to save you."

"They are busy killing your friends!"

"I doubt they'll get the chance." Frida kept the sword trained on Lady Craven and leaned into the cart. With her free hand, she typed something onto the keypad, as Jools had instructed. "You've just lost control."

The griefer queen eyed the screen and screeched. It read:

/gamemode 1

Frida hit ENTER.

Instantly, the nocturnal noises quieted. The zombie horde spreading over the hillside stopped moving forward and began milling about. Their moans now ended as a question: "Uuuuhh . . . *ooohhh?*"

Then cheering could be heard all the way from the portals. The zombies had broken off their chase. The cavalry troopers were safe. And the residents of Spike City would not be disturbed this night.

Frida's sword arm began to shake as she reached in to type again:

/kill

Lady Craven's gemstone eyes widened. She drew back against the wall of the minecart. But Frida did not complete the command.

She didn't have to. She had already thrown the griefer's game into Creative mode . . . and no hostile mobs would seek prey on anyone's orders.

Frida paused, and then gathered up Ocelot's reins and walked away from the minecart tracks. Killing Lady Craven here would not eliminate evil in the Overworld. Sooner or later, she'd figure out how to use her cheats to change modes again. She would come back to threaten Survival days and nights. And when she did, Battalion Zero would be there. That was the Overworld Frida and her friends knew and loved.

She touched the tattooed spot on the back of her neck as she picked her way back down the mountain, leading her mare. Surviving was no longer a solo quest and quitting no longer an option. Frida would fight to defend these biomes for everyone—forever, if she had to. Now that she knew why, there'd be no turning back. It was what she'd been born to do.

CHECK OUT THE REST OF THE DEFENDERS OF THE OVERWORLD SERIES

AND JOIN BATTALION ZERO'S QUEST:

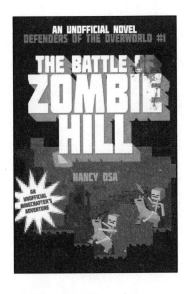

The Battle of
Zombie Hill

NANCY OSA

Spawn Point
Zero

NANCY OSA

DO YOU LIKE FICTION FOR MINECRAFTERS?

Check out other unofficial Minecrafter
adventures from Sky Pony Press!

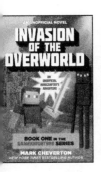

Invasion of the
Overworld

MARK CHEVERTON

Battle for the
Nether

MARK CHEVERTON

Confronting the
Dragon

MARK CHEVERTON

Trouble in
Zombie-town

MARK CHEVERTON

The Quest for
the Diamond
Sword

WINTER MORGAN

The Mystery
of the Griefer's
Mark

WINTER MORGAN

The Endermen
Invasion

WINTER MORGAN

Treasure
Hunters in
Trouble

WINTER MORGAN

Available wherever books are sold!